P9-CME-721

Duchess abruptly leaped to her feet and ran over to the door. She began to growl low in her throat.

Matt didn't waste a second. He grabbed his weapon. "Stay in the bedroom and don't open the door to anyone except for me or one of my brothers."

"Be careful," Lacy whispered.

Pressing himself against the wall, Matt carefully opened the door.

Duchess was in full alert mode, her nose practically twitching with the need to track the intruder. He exhaled and then darted outside, Duchess hot on his heels. As they'd practiced earlier, he went left and Duchess went right. He heard Duchess moving through the brush.

The dog let out a sharp bark, and he instinctively lunged toward the sound, his heart pounding with adrenaline. He moved from tree to tree. Suddenly a sharp crack echoed through the night, followed by a burning sensation along the outer edge of his left biceps.

He'd been shot!

Ignoring the pain, he continued his zigzagging path toward the area where Duchess had barked, alerting him to the presence of the gunman, as he silently prayed that he and Duchess could hold the guy off long enough for his brother Mike to arrive.

And to keep Lacy and Rory safe.

Laura Scott is a nurse by day and an author by night. She has always loved romance and read faith-based books by Grace Livingston Hill in her teenage years. She's thrilled to have published over twelve books for Love Inspired Suspense. She has two adult children and lives in Milwaukee, Wisconsin, with her husband of thirty years. Please visit Laura at laurascottbooks.com, as she loves to hear from her readers.

Visit the Author Profile page at Harlequin.com for more titles.

SHATTERED LULLABY

LAURA SCOTT

❖ HARLEQUIN® LOVE INSPIRED® SUSPENSE

If you purchased this book without a cover you should be aware that this book is stolen property. It was reported as "unsold and destroyed" to the publisher, and neither the author nor the publisher has received any payment for this "stripped book."

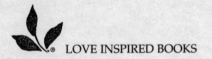

LOVE INSPIRED BOOKS

Recycling programs
for this product may
not exist in your area.

ISBN-13: 978-1-335-54349-3

Shattered Lullaby

Copyright © 2018 by Laura Iding

All rights reserved. Except for use in any review, the reproduction or utilization of this work in whole or in part in any form by any electronic, mechanical or other means, now known or hereinafter invented, including xerography, photocopying and recording, or in any information storage or retrieval system, is forbidden without the written permission of the editorial office, Love Inspired Books, 195 Broadway, New York, NY 10007 U.S.A.

This is a work of fiction. Names, characters, places and incidents are either the product of the author's imagination or are used fictitiously, and any resemblance to actual persons, living or dead, business establishments, events or locales is entirely coincidental.

This edition published by arrangement with Love Inspired Books.

® and TM are trademarks of Love Inspired Books, used under license. Trademarks indicated with ® are registered in the United States Patent and Trademark Office, the Canadian Intellectual Property Office and in other countries.

www.Harlequin.com

Printed in U.S.A.

Blessed are they that mourn: for they shall be comforted.
—Matthew 5:4

This book is dedicated to my cousin Joanne O'Connell. Thanks for all the awesome Tomahawk summer memories, especially teaching me how to water-ski!

ONE

Lacy Germaine woke to the sound of heated arguing. For a moment, she buried her head into the pillow in an effort to drown out her parents' fighting.

And then she remembered—her parents were long gone, both killed in a car crash several years ago. Abruptly, she sat bolt upright on the futon, her heart thundering in her chest.

One of the voices belonged to her sister, Jill, but who was she talking to?

Lacy leaped out of bed and went over to check on her three-month-old nephew, Rory, who was still sleeping, but not for long, considering the harsh tones coming from the next room.

At first the voices were low and angry but still incomprehensible. It didn't take long for the deeper male voice to rise. "Tell me the truth! Now! Or I'll kill you and the brat, too!"

Lacy sucked in a harsh breath, understanding with sick certainty that her sister's worst fears had become reality. Jill's husband, David Williams, had returned home.

And he was ambushing her sister after midnight.

Reacting instinctively, Lacy lifted her nephew from the crib and grabbed the long shawl-type wrap, winding it around and around, swaddling the baby snugly against her body. Then she fumbled for her cell phone and dialed 911.

"What's your emergency?"

"Domestic violence at 1671 Elmwood Lane," she whispered into the phone. "Hurry!"

"Please stay on the line," the woman responded calmly.

Lacy wanted to yell that this was her sister's life at stake! But of course she didn't.

"I can't. He'll hear me." Lacy disconnected from the call. She needed both of her hands free in order to manage the baby.

Her brother-in-law obviously didn't know Lacy was there, staying with Jill to help out over spring break. If he found out Jill wasn't alone...

She couldn't finish the thought.

"No, please..."

Lacy hated the idea of Jill begging for mercy. Her sister had confided that she was filing for divorce from her husband because his anger and verbal attacks scared her.

Clearly, Jill had been right. Lacy was getting

a firsthand idea of how frightening her brother-in-law could be.

"Please don't do this…" Her sister's voice was full of tears.

Bang! Bang!

No! Lacy gasped, her heart lodging in her throat. Dear God, what had David done?

There was nothing but silence after the gun went off, forcing Lacy to assume the worst.

Jill was dead. Shot by her own husband.

And if his threat was to be believed, Rory was next.

Lacy jammed her cell phone into her purse, slung the strap over her shoulder and shoved her feet into her running shoes. Where was the diaper bag?

In the kitchen.

Knowing she couldn't dare pass her sister's room to get the bag, she eased out from Rory's bedroom and darted around the corner in the opposite direction to go into the living room. She needed to get Rory out of the house, far away from his armed and dangerous father.

Thankfully, the patio doors slid open without a sound. She eased through into the mild April spring air. Relieved it wasn't too cold, she crossed the concrete patio until she reached the damp grass.

Grateful for the lack of snow, Lacy didn't

hesitate, running around the house and toward the road. Her car was parked less than a block from her sister's home, on the opposite side of the street, and she hoped she'd make it to the vehicle before David realized the baby was gone.

Mud squished beneath her running shoes. The warm spring weather had melted what was left of the snow, leaving mush behind. She slipped, then steadied herself.

Twenty yards, fifteen, ten. A loud thud from inside the house caused her to misstep, and this time she fell, one knee hitting the ground. Clutching the baby to her chest, she braced herself with one hand on the ground, surprised to feel a hard ridge beneath her fingertips. Some sort of key. Instinctively she picked it up and shoved it into the pocket of her hoodie as she leaped up to her feet.

Still holding the baby close with one hand, she fished in her purse for her car keys.

Five yards. Three. She was going to make it! Using her thumb, she pressed the key fob to unlock the driver's-side door. The car made an extraordinarily loud beeping noise, front and rear lights flashing. She winced, hoping David wouldn't hear. As if the car wasn't loud enough to broadcast her escape, Rory began to cry.

"Hey! Stop! Get back here!"

David's irate shout had her hunching her shoulders, half expecting to be hit with a bullet squarely in the back. Somehow, she managed to yank the driver's-side door open and to slide in behind the wheel. There was just enough room to maneuver with Rory bundled against her. She shut the door, jammed the key in the ignition and hit the accelerator, speeding away from her sister's house.

Lacy took a quick right and then a left, leaving the normally quiet neighborhood, expecting to hear the wail of sirens at any moment.

But there was nothing.

She'd called 911 for help, hadn't she? So where were the Milwaukee Police? How long would it take for them to show up?

What should she do? Even if the police would be there at any moment, Lacy didn't want to stop. What if David followed her? Every instinct she possessed told her to keep going, to put as much distance between herself and Rory's father as possible.

Think, Lacy, think! Where was the closest on-ramp? There! She found the sign and quickly took the ramp heading northwest, deeply afraid that David wasn't far behind.

No way would she allow him to lay one finger on Rory.

She would protect the baby with her own life if necessary. And she really, really hoped it wouldn't come to that.

Driving through the night, she kept her eyes peeled on the rearview mirror. She wished she could remember what kind of vehicle David drove, but she'd been focused only on escape, nothing more. She couldn't actually remember seeing any type of car, but David had to have driven to Jill's house in something. Her sister's house wasn't near a bus route.

Rory was still crying, signifying he was either hungry or needed his diaper changed, or both.

"Don't worry, I'll take care of you," she whispered in a soothing voice. Logically, she knew she should head to a police station, but nothing about this night made any rational sense.

And her sister's warnings echoed in her mind.

David's fellow police officers always cover for him; they believe whatever lies he's told them about me. Not one of them can be trusted.

At the time she'd thought Jill was being paranoid, but after this, she believed her sister had been right all along.

In fact, Jill had died because of it.

Tears welled in her eyes, blurring her vision. Lacy swiped them away, knowing she needed to be careful. In an effort to relax, she turned on the radio, searching for a soft jazz station, hoping the music would help calm Rory.

His crying had subsided to soft hiccupping sobs, the sound tearing at her heart. Keeping one hand on the wheel, she stroked his back as she drove, feeling guilty over not having him in a proper car seat. Driving with him in front of her was dangerous, but not as bad as staying behind where his father might try to kill him. Once again, her desperate need to flee wavered.

Should she turn around, go back to the police? But what if they were David's buddies? What if they didn't believe her?

If David succeeded in getting custody of Rory, what would prevent him from killing his son, the way he'd killed his wife?

No, she couldn't do it. She couldn't go back there. She had to wait until morning. There'd be plenty of time to find officers in another district far away from the one where David worked, who would listen to her side of the story. Surely they would believe her.

A weird beeping sound came from the radio, but before she could reach over to change the station, she heard the announcement of an Amber Alert.

"Missing three-month-old boy, Rory Williams, believed to be in a blue sedan belonging to his aunt, Lacy Germaine. The woman who took the child is in her late twenties and has long blond hair. Please call the Milwaukee Police Department if you see anyone matching this description."

Lacy tightened her grip on the steering wheel,

feeling sick to her stomach. How was it possible that there was an Amber Alert so soon? Why would the police be looking for her and Rory? What had happened at her sister's house when the police had arrived? Had David played the role of grieving husband and father? Had he found a way to place the blame for what had happened to Jill on someone else?

On her?

She hadn't prayed in a long time, since before her parents had died. But desperate times called for extreme measures so she sent up a quick request, hoping God would care about an innocent baby.

Help me keep this child safe.

A sense of calm settled over her, slowing her breathing, but she still needed a plan. She took the next exit on the freeway and began searching for a convenience store. Rory began crying again and she knew she couldn't wait a moment longer. She needed diapers and formula, both essentials in caring for an infant. Good thing she still had one of Rory's bottles in her purse from their earlier outing to the park.

Once she found a safe place to stay and had the baby changed and fed, she would think about what she would do next. There must be a police department she could go to in order to turn herself in. A district that wouldn't believe David's lies.

Catching a glimpse of bright lights up ahead, she gratefully headed toward the store attached to a gas station. She pulled up to a pump and quickly filled her tank. She didn't have a lot of cash, however, forcing her to use a credit card, but having enough fuel was worth the risk. She knew the police would track her this far, but hopefully she'd be long gone before they could send a squad car to come pick her up.

She walked into the store and began searching the shelves for what she would need. There was a short, rotund man with a long scraggly beard behind the counter. He watched her like a hawk through thick, dark-rimmed glasses. Was he expecting her to steal something?

Or worse, had he heard the Amber Alert?

Praying it wasn't the latter, she tried to act natural, idly perusing the shelves, searching for the items she needed. She could feel the round bearded guy's gaze piercing her back, like tiny laser beams.

She tucked a package of diapers beneath her arm, then shifted a few steps to the right, looking over the various types of formula on display. Recognizing the yellow canister her sister used, she picked that one up.

Bright lights flashed through the window, startling her so much that she jumped a little. She cast a fugitive glance over her shoulder. Had the police found her already? She hesitated, wondering if she should just leave and go somewhere else.

The front door of the shop opened, and it took every ounce of strength she possessed not to turn and stare at whoever had come inside. She slid around the row of shelving, putting distance between herself and the newcomer.

A glimpse of black hair beneath a dark hat caught her eye and she ducked farther down, her pulse skipping several beats.

David had black hair. But he couldn't possibly have found her so quickly. Right?

She didn't want to believe it. Couldn't imagine how. Her sister's husband might have been a Special Ops soldier at one point, but he wasn't Superman.

Just her worst nightmare.

She tucked the canister of formula into the folds of the baby wrap and slipped a twenty-dollar bill from her purse, leaving it on the shelf to pay for the items she'd taken. Then she eased around another row of supplies, slowly making her way toward the main doorway.

After painstakingly slow maneuvering, she finally had a clear pathway to the door. Praying for safety, she took a deep breath, tucked her head and made a run for it.

Heading home after a long double shift, Officer Matthew Callahan and his K-9 partner, a tall German shepherd named Duchess, came upon a convenience store located six blocks from the church the Callahan family had attended ever since he could remember. His stomach rumbled with hunger, and since he knew there wasn't much food at home, he decided to stop for a bite to eat.

As he pulled into the parking lot, his headlights shined on a tall woman with long blond hair holding something bulky beneath her arm, running in a full-out sprint for the navy blue sedan sitting next to a gas pump.

What in the world?

Matt threw the gearshift into Park, hit the button to lift the tailgate so Duchess could jump down and then bolted from the vehicle.

Before he could yell at the woman to stop, he saw another tall man, a black cap covering his head, coming out of the convenience store, obviously following her. At first, Matt thought he was another cop, especially when he saw the gun in the guy's hand.

But then he lifted his weapon and aimed it directly toward the fleeing woman without warning.

"Stop! Police! Drop your weapon!" Matt shouted, turning his attention to the armed man. "Duchess, Attack!"

The man wearing the cap glanced over in alarm, lowered his gun and quickly took off behind the store with Duchess in hot pursuit. With the gunman covered, he went after the woman.

"Oh, no, you don't," he said, grabbing a hold of her before she could get into her navy blue four-door. "What's going on here? What happened inside the store?"

"Let me go! Didn't you see that man back there?" she demanded. "He's trying to kill me and the baby!"

Since he'd seen that much for himself, Matt couldn't deny her statement held merit. Still, something about this entire scenario seemed off. "Who is he? What's his name?"

Before she could respond, his K-9 partner let out a yelp of pain.

Instantly he spun on his heel, alarm skittering through him. "Duchess!"

The dog came running toward him, her coat glistening with something wet and shiny. Then he noticed the blood trail behind her.

"Oh, no, he hurt your dog!" The woman said in alarm.

Duchess came up to rest against his leg. He reached down and saw there was a long lacera-tion in her side, most likely from a knife. Thank-fully, it didn't look too deep.

"Please don't arrest me," she said in a low voice. "My name is Lacy and I'm a schoolteacher on spring break. You need to understand that man is my brother-in-law, and he shot and killed my sister. Rory is my nephew and I heard him threaten to kill his son, the same way he murdered my sister. Please, you have to believe me!"

Oddly enough, Matt was leaning toward believing her. Not just because he'd watched that man point a gun at the woman, but also because he had lashed out at his partner. He glanced down at Duchess, who was still bleeding, and made a split-second decision. "Fine, but you're coming with me."

"No, wait…"

"Now!" Matt wasn't in the mood to quibble. He needed to get his partner's injury taken care of, and since this woman and the baby were also clearly in danger, he decided it was better to take them along.

He would figure out what to do with them later.

"Okay, but we need to hurry," she said.

Lacy surprised him by gathering up her items—baby things, he belatedly realized, such as diapers and formula—then heading over to his SUV without waiting for him.

Once she made up her mind about something, clearly, she acted on it. It was a trait he couldn't help but admire.

"Come on, Duchess." He led his partner back to the SUV and lifted her inside. Opening the first-aid kit he kept on hand for just these types of emergencies, Matt quickly pressed several gauze pads over the gash in her coat to stop the bleeding, then wrapped gauze around her abdomen as an added precaution. Duchess was trained well enough to leave the field dressing alone.

Satisfied he'd done what he could for the moment, he leaned over and rested his face against the animal's neck. "You're going to be okay, hear me? I'll get this taken care of right away."

Duchess licked his face, making him smile. He stepped back and closed the tailgate.

Gunfire erupted from the far east corner of the store, the same place where the gunman had disappeared. A bullet shattered the plastic sign hanging just over his head.

Matt didn't waste another moment. He jumped in behind the wheel and started the engine with a roar.

His tires screeched loudly as he drove away from the gas station. Once the lights from the store faded to nothing, he glanced in the rearview mirror at his passengers. He hated leaving the scene of the crime, but at the same time, Duchess's needs came first.

While he thought it was odd Lacy had chosen to sit in the back seat, he'd barely gotten onto the interstate when he saw the electric sign over the freeway blinking with the news of an Amber Alert.

The description on the sign matched the woman and baby sitting behind him.

He ground his teeth together, knowing this case was getting more complicated by the minute.

Somehow, some way, he needed to keep this woman and baby safe while he figured out what in the world was going on.

He couldn't bear the thought of losing another innocent child...

TWO

Lacy took a deep breath, desperately hoping she hadn't made a mistake going along with this cop. The fact that he was a K-9 officer irrationally soothed her fears.

Which was crazy and completely illogical. Anyone could have bad blood running through their veins. Her brother-in-law, Officer David Williams, was proof of that. He'd been so nice, so charming in the beginning.

But it soon became apparent that his niceness had been nothing but a facade hiding his cold black heart.

"Dispatch, this is Unit Twenty-one reporting gunfire at the Gas and Go store located on Bradley and Markwell. Send units out to that location. The perp who was last seen there injured my K-9 partner. He's roughly six feet tall wearing all black, including a dark cap over his head."

"Ten-four, Unit Twenty-one. Will send units

to respond. What's your partner's status? Aren't you off duty?"

"I was off duty, but interrupted a crime in progress. I'm taking my partner in to be seen at the emergency vet. The perp tried to run, which is when my K-9 partner was injured." He glanced at her in the rearview mirror, then continued, "I'll write up my report as soon as my partner has been cared for."

"Ten-four."

Lacy let out her breath in a silent sigh. She'd wondered if the cop would mention her and Rory since David had clearly been after her, not the dog. And what about the Amber Alert? She knew this cop must have known about it. Or was it possible he'd missed the news since he was off duty?

The minute the thought entered her mind, she saw the Amber Alert flashing on the electric sign over the interstate.

Busted.

Rory was still crying, so she focused on caring for the baby. Since she was already breaking rules by not having him in a car seat, she decided to go ahead and get him changed. It was part of the reason she'd chosen the back seat. If she'd had water she would have made a bottle of formula for him, too. She should have thought of picking some up at the store.

So far, she was doing a lousy job of taking care

of her young nephew. Not that she had much experience with babies. She taught fifth grade, not preschool.

"Shh, it's okay, Rory. Auntie Lacy is here. You're going to be fine. It's okay," she continued talking to the baby, who continued to wail. She glanced up at the officer, hoping he wasn't the type to lose his temper over a crying infant.

What did she really know about him? Other than he cared about his dog?

She deftly changed Rory, then bundled him back up in the sling, hoping he would calm down enough to fall back asleep.

Not hardly.

"Maybe the kid is hungry?" the officer suggested.

She stifled a sigh. "I'm well aware of that fact. I have a can of powdered formula from the store, but it's useless without water."

"I have bottled water." He rummaged beneath the passenger seat and pulled out a fresh bottle of water, handing it to her over his shoulder. "I always keep a case in the SUV for my dog, Duchess."

"Thank you." The water wasn't warm, but it wasn't cold, either. Hopefully, he'd take it without a problem.

She made Rory's bottle, shaking the thing with enough force to make her teeth rattle in an effort to be sure the powder was completely dissolved. Then she shifted the baby in her arms so that she could feed him.

Rory latched onto the nipple with the strength of a linebacker. Apparently he was too hungry to care if the water bottle was warm or not.

With a sigh of relief, she gazed into Rory's wide eyes. This poor baby was in danger for no reason other than his father was an abusive, controlling lunatic.

She squeezed her eyes shut and lowered her mouth to press a kiss against the top of his downy head. He smelled like baby shampoo, and she had to fight against another wave of tears.

No child should have to grow up without his mother. Or with the knowledge that his father had killed his mother.

A sense of hopelessness hit hard, and she forced herself to shove it aside. Self-pity wasn't going to help.

She needed to remain strong, for Rory's sake.

Rory released his viselike grip on the bottle, so she lifted him up to her shoulder and lightly rubbed his back in slow circular motions. Duchess stuck her nose through the crate, pressing it along the back of Lacy's neck, making her smile.

Rory let out a wet belch and she instantly praised him. "Good boy! Yes, you're such a good boy!"

He lifted his head from her shoulder and smiled up at her with a toothless grin. She kissed him again, then turned him so that his head rested in the crook of her arm. As he finished the rest of the bottle, she glanced up and caught the officer staring at her through the rearview mirror.

"Where are we going?" she asked.

"To a twenty-four hour veterinary service," he answered. "Why don't you tell me exactly what took place tonight?"

"Look, Officer," she began, but he quickly interrupted.

"Matt. My name is Matthew Callahan."

Matt was a nice name, one that carried an inner strength. She shook her head quickly. She was acting irrational again. As if a name mattered. Wasn't David the one in the Bible who took down Goliath with a slingshot? It didn't mean her sister's husband was a good man.

Quite the opposite.

She gave herself a mental shake. "Okay, Matt. I'm sure you've figured out by now that I'm Lacy Germaine, and this baby is Rory Williams. There's an Amber Alert out on the baby and I understand we're in your custody."

"Is that why you chose to sit in the back seat?" he asked.

"No." Not only had she wanted to change Rory, but she secretly preferred being closer to the dog than to him. She forced herself to stay on track. "I've been staying at my sister's house for a few days to help her with Rory. I woke up to the sound of arguing and heard my sister begging not to be hurt. Before this happened, she had told me she was afraid of her husband, David Williams, because of his temper. In fact, she recently filed for divorce. He was clearly angry about that—I overheard him threaten to kill her and Rory, too, right before I heard two gunshots. And the biggest problem of all is that David Williams is a police officer working in the third district."

"He's a cop?" Matt demanded, his expression turning grim.

"Yes." She could already tell that he didn't want to believe her. "When I heard them arguing, I called 911 and gave the dispatcher my sister's address. Then I took off with Rory."

"So why the Amber Alert?"

Rory had fallen asleep, the bottle just about empty, so she pulled it away and set it aside. "I don't know. I can only assume that David somehow convinced his cop buddies that I'm the one who killed Jill and took Rory. Which doesn't make any sense."

He snorted in derision. "I'll say. Even a rookie would have a hard time buying that story. There has to be something else going on."

She clenched her jaw. "I don't know what else

is going on. You saw that David had a gun, didn't you? And he took a slice out of Duchess. What more do you want from me? I can't tell you what I don't know!"

Rory shifted restlessly in her arms, and she mentally berated herself for raising her voice. Rory shouldn't have to listen to her arguing with a cop. He'd had enough exposure to violence in his short life.

She let out a sigh and stroked the tip of her finger over his plump cheek. Now that Jill was gone, it would be up to her to take care of Rory. To raise him as her own.

To love him.

She swallowed a sense of panic. Okay, she didn't know much about babies, but that didn't mean she couldn't take a crash course to learn.

Lacy silently promised to give Rory the stable life he deserved.

Matt didn't understand why he was so captivated by Lacy taking care of Rory. He came from a large family, sure, but he wasn't like his two eldest brothers, Marc and Miles, who'd both married women with children.

Truthfully, he'd gone down that path with devastating results. He'd begun dating a divorced woman named Debra who had a four-year-old daughter, Carly. He'd been about to propose when

Carly had gotten sick and had been diagnosed with a rare form of lethal cancer. During the next few months, he'd been forced to watch the child he'd come to love die a horrible death. On top of that, the crisis had caused Debra and her ex-husband, Kyle, to grow close again. After Carly's death, Debra had broken up with Matt, claiming she and Kyle were going to reunite.

Logically, he knew he should have been happy for them, but he'd felt Carly's loss as keenly as they had. Losing a child, even one who wasn't his by blood, had been the most painful thing he'd ever experienced. Debra's rejection afterward hadn't helped.

When Debra walked away, he'd decided it was easier to avoid romantic entanglements and to focus on his career. Dogs were better than people any day of the week. He'd loved K-9 training, and Duchess made the best partner he could have imagined. He still had the closeness he shared with his twin, Maddy, and was truly happy she'd found love with his former partner, Noah Sinclair.

Using the rearview mirror, he kept a close eye on his partner. If his gaze strayed on occasion to Lacy and the baby, he quickly caught himself and looked away. He didn't need to keep an eye on his passengers, as Duchess seemed to be enthralled by the woman and the baby in the back seat.

Or maybe his partner instinctively knew to offer her protection.

He grappled with Lacy's allegation that the dark-haired guy was a police officer. He could easily find out for sure, but he was loath to use his radio. He'd bought them a little time, but he couldn't postpone the inevitable forever. Now that he knew about the Amber Alert, he would have to take Lacy and Rory into custody so she could provide her side of the story.

In his gut, he believed she was telling the truth. But he also knew that David's being a cop would make things a lot more difficult.

Her word against that of a police officer.

He didn't like it.

Even worse, he wasn't sure he'd be able to continue investigating the case. In theory, once he handed her over, his role in this mess would be finished. The case would be given to one of the homicide detectives, not a K-9 officer.

The thought was depressing. Matt didn't want to become attached to the little guy, but at the same time, he worried about what would happen to him. The kid was the real innocent victim here. Would he end up in foster care?

Maybe, but it was likely a whole lot better than ending up with his father.

The lights from the emergency veterinary clinic loomed up ahead, so he turned in that direction.

He and Duchess had only been there once before, and that was related to another on-the-job
injury. Some perp had kicked Duchess in the head
and he'd panicked, fearing she had suffered some
sort of brain injury. She'd been fine, and he was
determined she would get through this latest injury without complications as well.

After parking the SUV, he jumped out and
went around to the back to get Duchess. She
lifted her head, her tail thumping in greeting,
but he could tell by the way she was acting that
the wound along her side hurt.

"It's okay, girl. I have you." He scooped the animal into his arms—no small feat since she was
a solid German shepherd weighing in at eighty
pounds, hefty for a female.

She licked his face again and he used his elbow
to close the back hatch. As he rounded the corner of the SUV, he realized that Lacy had gotten
out of the vehicle with Rory swaddled against
her. She held the door to the clinic open for him.

"Thanks," he said, carrying Duchess inside.

"You're welcome." She surprised him again by
following him into the building.

He supposed it was better for her to be inside
the building since her brother-in-law was looking
for her.It bothered him to think about her need
to escape with Rory in the middle of the night.

He focused on Duchess. Blood was seeping

through the dressings he'd applied, so he looked around for someone to talk to. "I need some help here," he said in a loud tone.

The veterinary assistant came out of the back, then hurried over. "What happened?"

"This is my K-9 partner. She was cut by a sharp object," he said. "The laceration is roughly six inches long."

"This way." The assistant led the way through a door into a small exam room.

He eased the dog down on the stainless steel table, disconcerted to realize that Lacy had followed him again. Why her actions distracted him, he had no idea. Maybe on some level, he expected her to take off with the baby. In fact, he couldn't even say he would blame her if she did.

But she didn't.

The vet, a tall man who appeared to be in his early fifties, entered the room. After washing his hands in the corner sink, he approached Duchess. "I'm Dr. Hogan. Do you have any idea what was used to cause the laceration?"

"No, it was dark. I assume a knife, but couldn't say for sure." Matt stayed near Duchess, holding her in place, stroking the soft fur between her ears reassuringly. "Her name is Duchess and she's a K-9 officer."

"Hi, Duchess." The vet spoke in a soothing

voice. He glanced at Matt. "I assume her shots are up to date?"

"Yes." Matt watched as the vet cut through the gauze he'd wrapped around the dog's torso.

"Well, I'm glad to see the cut isn't too deep," Dr. Hogan said. "I think we can close it up with glue. Hopefully, it won't bother her too much."

The huge wave of guilt rolled off his back. Duchess really would be okay.

"She'll need some antibiotics, since we don't know what cut her, along with some pain meds." Dr. Hogan lifted his gaze to Matt's. "First, we'll get this cleaned up, okay?"

He nodded again, grateful that his partner wouldn't need surgery. He sent up a silent prayer of thanks to God for watching over them.

Praying came natural to him. Growing up in the Callahan family meant they went to church every Sunday, followed by brunch at his mother's home. His father, Max Callahan, the former Chief of Police, had died in the line of duty over two years ago, but in some ways it felt as if the event that had so dramatically changed their lives had happened yesterday.

The perp who'd shot his father had never been caught, a fact that nagged at him incessantly. And he knew it bothered the rest of his brothers and his twin sister, too. He'd spent some time trying to investigate the case but had gotten sidetracked when he'd been selected for K-9 training.

His father had instilled a sense of serving the community in all six of his children. Most of them had gone into some type of law enforcement work; Marc was an FBI agent, Miles a homicide detective, Mitch an arson investigator, and Matt's twin, Maddy, a lawyer, working in the DA's office. Only his middle brother, Mike, had defied his father's wishes by becoming a private investigator.

"Matt?" Lacy's soft voice interrupted his thoughts. "I'm glad Duchess is going to be okay."

"Thanks." He forced a smile. "Me, too."

She took the baby bottle she'd used to feed Rory and washed it out in the sink. He couldn't help but admire how she managed to take care of an infant in less than optimal conditions.

The veterinary assistant came in with a razor and a bowl of soapy water. For the next five minutes, he held Duchess in place while the assistant first trimmed the dog's fur from the area around the laceration, then used the soapy water to clean it. By the time they were finished, Matt's uniform was almost as wet as Duchess's coat.

"Dr. Hogan will be back shortly," the assistant said, emptying the bowl of soapy water into the sink, then rinsing it out.

An hour later, Duchess was ready to go. She

took her antibiotics and pain pills in a ball of peanut butter like a pro. Since the leash was out in the car and he didn't want Duchess to pull on the glue the vet had used to close her incision, he once again scooped her into his arms.

Lacy went ahead to open the doors for him as they made their way back outside. The moon was high in the sky, and even though he was certain they hadn't been followed, the tiny hairs along the back of his neck lifted and pricked in warning.

"Take the baby and get inside," he said, once she'd opened the back hatch.

Lacy quickly scooted into the back seat. He closed the door behind Duchess, then hurried behind the wheel.

Twin headlights pierced the night, and he quickly started the engine and backed out of the parking spot. The headlights grew closer, and he couldn't ignore a sliver of apprehension.

Should he call for backup? Or was he being paranoid? Probably the latter, so he headed away from the lights, in the opposite direction. At two in the morning, he didn't expect there to be much traffic on the road.

The twin headlights followed.

He glanced in his rearview mirror at Lacy holding the baby and Duchess stretched out in the back. No way was he going to risk becoming involved in some sort of high-speed car chase.

Grabbing the radio, he quickly called it in. "Dispatch, this is Unit Twenty-one, requesting backup at my current location, about five miles away from the emergency veterinary clinic, heading westbound on interstate ninety-four."

"Ten-four, what's the problem?"

He wasn't exactly sure how to phrase his concerns. "I appear to have picked up a tail, and my partner is temporarily out of commission."

"Unit Five is only a few miles away. He should catch up with you shortly."

"Thanks." He disconnected from the radio, needing both hands on the wheel. The headlights grew brighter as the vehicle behind him began to close the gap.

Was it possible the guy dressed in black, David Williams, had come to finish what he'd started? Matt gave himself a mental kick. He shouldn't have announced over the radio that he was taking Duchess to the emergency vet. As a cop, Williams likely had a radio in his vehicle. Process of elimination would have made finding him and Lacy way too easy. There were only two emergency veterinary hospitals offering services around the clock in the area.

Swallowing hard, Matt pushed the speed as high as he dared, considering his precious cargo. Even though Lacy was wearing her seat belt, she didn't have the proper infant car seat for Rory, and he knew if they were hit hard enough, there was a chance she could lose her grip on the baby.

And Duchess wasn't up to par, either, considering she'd been given antibiotics and pain meds.

The headlights grew impossibly brighter. Was Williams gaining ground?

Where was his backup?

The headlights abruptly shifted, going into the left lane, coming up on his driver's side. Matt did his best not to panic. He decided to wait until the guy was almost upon him before he would abruptly slow down, hoping the guy would shoot past them.

"This is a good time to pray," he told Lacy. She looked surprised by his comment. "I'm serious. I know God will watch over us, and we need all the help we can get."

She gave a terse nod, then began reciting the "Our Father" prayer, which made him wonder if she wasn't used to praying on the fly.

"Dear Lord, give me the strength to keep us all safe," he murmured as the lights grew brighter and brighter.

Soon they were almost parallel to his rear bumper.

Now!

He took his foot off the gas and pressed gently on the brake. The vehicle flew past him, and he didn't waste another moment. Wrenching the wheel to the left, he drove his SUV across the median, crossed the three lanes that were thankfully absent of traffic, and took the next exit he could find.

It was several miles before he could relax enough to breathe normally. But the close call bothered him.

At the moment, he didn't feel confident enough to take Lacy and Rory to the police station. They would be far too vulnerable there. He didn't want them anywhere near a place where the ex-husband who happened to be a cop could find them.

Nope. What he needed was a new plan.

There had to be some way to keep Lacy and Rory safe from harm while he tracked down the guy intent on killing them.

THREE

Lacy clutched Rory close, determined to hang on to him no matter what happened. She closed her eyes, the scenery flashing past the window making her dizzy. Duchess didn't much like the rocky ride, either, whining a bit and scrambling to regain her balance.

"Sorry, Duchess," Matt muttered.

Once again, she was oddly reassured by how much Matt cared about his dog. Not to mention that he'd told her now was a good time to pray. And most important, how he'd looked so concerned when he'd carried the animal in and out of the emergency vet clinic.

Surely, a guy who loved dogs couldn't be all bad.

After what seemed like forever but was probably less than twenty minutes, Matt spoke up from the front seat. "Sorry about the bumpy ride. Are you and the baby okay?"

"F-fine." Her breath hitched in her chest and

she fought the urge to break down sobbing. When would this nightmare end? Why was David doing this?

Nothing made any sense.

"I've lost him for now," Matt continued. "You're safe."

She shook her head, knowing she and Rory wouldn't be safe until somehow the authorities found David and arrested him. "He won't stop," she said in a low voice. "Jill told me that David is a terrible control freak. Who knows what horrible things he's capable of."

"I'm getting a pretty good idea," Matt said, his tone grim. "Apparently he doesn't mind taking out a fellow officer in his quest to get at his son."

"Not just his son, but me, too." She tried to think of a way to make him understand. "Not just because I'm Jill's sister, but he caught a glimpse of me taking off in my car. So he knows I'm a witness to her murder. My testimony could put him away for the rest of his life."

"I know and I believe you. I totally get that the guy is a serious head case. I need to call my lieutenant, but can't risk using the radio just yet."

The thought of Matt calling his boss made her stomach clench. "Please don't. Don't turn me into the authorities."

His gaze met hers in the rearview mirror. "I have to. When I explain what I know, my boss

will call off the Amber Alert and put a BOLO—
Be On the Lookout—on David Williams instead.
Trust me, they'll find him and arrest him. You
and the baby will be safe."

Having David locked up in jail was something
she wanted more than anything, but she wouldn't
be able to rest until she knew he'd been appre-
hended.

"It's so late. Can't you give me a little time?"
She tried not to sound as if she were begging,
even though she would if necessary. "Rory needs
some rest. He's been through a lot over the past
few hours."

"I know." Once again his gaze briefly met hers.
"And so have you."

She didn't want to think about the fact that her
sister was gone. Everything that had taken place
seemed surreal. As if she might wake up in the
morning to discover this was all nothing more
than a bad dream.

"Yes," she agreed. "Both of us could use some
time to rest and regroup."

There was a long silence before Matt spoke
again. "Duchess could use a few hours off as
well, so I'll find someplace to rest for what's left
of the night. I'll report in to my boss first thing
tomorrow morning."

Since it was already nearing 2:30 a.m., she

didn't find that too reassuring. How many hours of rest would he give her? Five or six at the most?

Not nearly enough, but at this point she told herself to take what she could get. "Thank you."

"You're welcome."

The vehicle slowed and made a right-hand turn. She noticed that he'd pulled up to a motel with a bright *Vacancy* sign. She sat up straighter, keeping one hand against Rory, wondering if they had a crib available.

"This place will take cash from cops and they're pet-friendly," he said as he threw the gearshift into Park. "Two of my brothers are cops and have used this place to keep people safe before."

Brothers? Plural? A sense of unease niggled beneath her skin. What if one of them was friends with David Williams? What if they found a way to convince Matt that she was the guilty one, not David?

Why had she assumed she was safe with this particular cop? So what if he loved his dog? She still didn't know anything about him.

Except for the fact that he'd told her it was a good time to pray.

She didn't really know any men who actually prayed. Oh, sure, her father used to take them to church, but it was nothing more than an act. In private, he was anything but loving. Going to church had only been to make them look good in the community.

Sad to think that Jill had married a man who was exactly like their father.

Duchess pressed her nose against the back of Lacy's neck again, as if sensing her distress. She liked the dog better than she liked the master. The adrenaline rush had faded, leaving a nagging headache in its wake. Maybe that's why she was having trouble thinking clearly. Who could concentrate after witnessing a murder, being shot at and then followed?

"Stay inside for a moment," Matt said. "I'll see if I can get us adjoining rooms."

"Ask for a crib," she interjected before he could slam the door.

"Oh, yeah. Sure."

She rested back against the seat cushion, shivering in the night. A blanket of exhaustion dropped over her, and she had almost drifted off to sleep when Matt returned.

"We're all set." Matt slid in behind the wheel. "We have two adjoining rooms, one with a crib. The crib should be set up by the time we get inside."

"That's great, thanks." The fact that he'd gotten adjoining rooms was reassuring. Maybe his kindness wasn't just an act.

Matt drove around the motel and pulled up in

front of two rooms on the ground floor, which would make caring for Duchess much easier.

After parking, Matt jumped out and opened the door for her. He offered his hand to help her out, and she took it, all too aware of the warmth of his fingers against hers. She dropped his hand, feeling self-conscious.

He used the key to open the door to room ten, then flipped on the light switch and handed her the key. She took Rory inside, grateful to see that there was in fact a crib in the room, set up near the bathroom.

The door closed behind her. She crossed over and gently began unwrapping the swaddling cloth that she'd used as an infant carrier. Rory squirmed, sighed and then quieted down again as she set him on his back in the crib.

For a long moment she stared down at his sleeping face, trying to find solace in the fact that he was too young to remember any of this.

A blessing, except for the fact that he would never know his mother. Fresh tears burned behind her eyelids, and she swiped them away and turned back into the room.

Rory wouldn't be alone. He'd always have her. She'd care for him the way she knew Jill would want her to. She wasn't sure how she would manage, but she would find a way.

There was a light tapping on the connecting

door. Flipping back the dead bolt, she opened it up to see Matt standing there holding her purse, the diapers and the formula, with Duchess at his side. "I brought in your things."

"Thanks." She stepped back, giving him room to enter. He set everything down on the small desk, and she stole a glance at him. He was handsome, his mink brown hair longer than what most cops sported, with brilliant green eyes. He wasn't that much taller than her own five feet and eight inches, but he was broad across the shoulders in a way that made her feel smaller than she really was.

No question, Matt looked as if he could have his pick of women. If you liked a man in uniform.

Good thing she wasn't a fan. In her experience, macho men like her father and brother-in-law were the ones to stay far away from.

Although if she were honest, she had to admit that Matt didn't act like her father or brother-in-law. Still, she wasn't going to take anything at face value. Not anymore.

She crossed her arms over her chest in a defensive gesture. "Will you talk to me before you call your boss?"

He lifted a brow. "Sure, if that's what you want."

"I'd appreciate it." Duchess moved over to sniff at the crib, then returned to stand beside Matt.

The dog was more gold than black, the long laceration on her right side an aberration against her glossy coat.

"Let me know if you need anything," Matt said, moving back toward the connecting door. "And leave your side unlocked in case anything happens, okay?"

She gave him a terse nod. "Good night."

"Good night."

When he and Duchess left the room, she made sure the connecting door remained ajar as he'd asked before dousing the light and crawling beneath the covers fully dressed.

Sleep should have come easily, but for some reason her mind decided to replay the events of the past few hours. She pressed the pillow over her ears, as if that would help silence her sister's pleas. The subsequent gunshots.

Deafening silence.

She must have slept a little because Rory's crying woke up her up at quarter to six in the morning. Bleary-eyed, she dragged herself out of bed, stumbling a bit as she went over to make him a bottle.

She should have made it the night before. That's probably what Jill would have done. Using warm water from the tap, she made his bottle, then quickly changed his diaper.

It was messy, and of course she'd completely

forgotten about picking up wet wipes. The wash-cloth from the bathroom seemed too rough against his skin, but it did the trick. Finally, she had him changed and settled in the crook of her arm with the bottle.

She eased down onto the bed and closed her eyes, feeling like a failure. Being a mother wasn't as instinctive as she'd hoped. What else had she forgotten? The poor thing didn't even have a change of clothes.

She kissed the top of his head. "It's just you and me, kiddo. Just you and me." Hopefully, she and Rory would be able to figure things out, to-gether.

Matt groaned when he heard the baby crying, tempted to bury his head into the pillow to drown out the noise.

Although if Lacy was up, then he should be awake, too. He squinted at the clock, realizing it was barely six.

He needed to talk to his boss, his lieutenant, not his shift commander, but he wouldn't be in until eight o'clock. A full two hours from now.

Beside him, Duchess thumped her tail and lifted her head as if asking if it was time to get up.

"Easy girl," he soothed, lightly scratching her between the ears. "You need your rest."

Duchess licked his wrist, then set her head

back down on the mattress. Propping himself up on his elbow, he gently palpated the long laceration. The wound looked decent, considering what she'd been through. Still, she'd carry the scar with her always.

A fresh burst of anger hit hard. Not just because of Duchess's injury, but on behalf of the woman and baby next door. That guy had killed his wife and had tried to kill a woman and her baby, not caring that he'd almost taken out two police officers.

Yeah, capturing David Williams and putting him behind bars was definitely at the top of his list of priorities. He'd have to find a way to convince his boss to let him assist in the investigation.

The crying next door subsided, but even in the silence, he couldn't fall back asleep. Dragging himself upright, he walked over to the window next to the door and pushed the curtain aside to sweep his gaze over the area. Convinced that nothing seemed out of place, he gestured for Duchess to come.

His partner ambled up and lightly jumped from the bed. He didn't carry her this time, needing to understand what she was able to do. Being the trooper she was, she moved as gracefully as ever, the pain from the incision apparently not bad enough to hold her back.

"Good girl," he praised, giving her a treat from his pocket. Deciding to leave her off leash, he pulled on his jacket and took her outside.

He was making his way back across the parking lot when the door to Lacy's room burst open. She had the baby wrapped against her with the cloth thingy, but the expression in her eyes was full of panic.

He immediately broke into a run, heading straight toward her, Duchess keeping pace at his side. "What is it? What's wrong?" He looked for signs of an intruder.

"I— Nothing, sorry. I thought you were leaving me behind." Her cheeks went pink and she averted her gaze.

"No, of course not." He was relieved there was nothing seriously wrong. He took her arm and drew her back inside the room, closing the door behind them. "I told you I wouldn't call my boss without talking to you first. He won't be in until closer to eight o'clock."

Her smile was weak as she dropped back down on the edge of the bed. "I'm sorry to overreact like that. It's just…" she shrugged. "Realizing that I'm all Rory has left in the world is a little overwhelming."

The baby was wide-awake, lifting his head and looking around with large curious blue eyes. Matt hadn't really understood until this moment just how big of a change this was for Lacy. The reality of her situation was clearly just sinking in.

"Looks like he's going to be up for a while. Should we find something to eat?"

Her tenuous smile widened, but then she grimaced. "That sounds great. Except for the fact that I don't have a car seat for Rory. I'm not sure I can manage a restaurant without one."

"Okay, how about I pick something up and bring it back? There's a family restaurant a few blocks from here. Tell me what you like."

"Scrambled eggs, wheat toast and bacon," she said. "Looks like the motel provides coffee in the room."

She had ordered exactly what he'd planned to get, which made him smile. "Yeah, but the pot only makes one cup. I'll get us both coffee to go, too." He turned toward his room, then looked back at Duchess. "Stay, Duchess. Guard."

Duchess instantly dropped to her haunches, sitting straight and tall. Lacy reached out to pet her, and he bit back a protest. It was clear Lacy was feeling emotionally fragile at the moment, and it wouldn't hurt for Duchess to get a little extra attention.

The trip to and from the restaurant didn't take long, but he didn't like leaving them alone. Duchess would protect Lacy and Rory with her life, but she wasn't bulletproof, either.

And he suspected that next time, David Williams wouldn't bother using a knife. In fact, he was surprised but glad he hadn't used his gun against Duchess.

Matt entered the motel through his room, then knocked on the connecting door that was still ajar. "Food's here," he called.

"Come on in."

Duchess greeted him with her usual tail wag, and he had to admit he loved that she was always happy to see him. Lacy had cleaned off the small desk so he could set the insulated containers down. He smiled when he realized she'd brewed herself a cup of coffee.

He pulled the two chairs over as Lacy set Rory back in the crib. Duchess went over and stretched out on the carpet in front of the crib, as if knowing it was her job to protect the baby.

"Duchess is amazing," Lacy said, dropping into the chair beside him. "Thanks for picking up breakfast."

"Yes, my partner is awesome, and you're welcome." He bowed his head and began to pray. "Dear Lord, we thank You for this food we are about to eat and for Your continued guidance and protection as we seek safety. Amen."

There was a brief pause before Lacy added, "Amen."

"Dig in," he teased, thinking about how they'd

always said those words after their family prayer when growing up.

Lacy picked up her plastic fork and dug into her eggs. "Do you always pray like that?" she asked.

He bit into a crisp piece of bacon, glancing at her in surprise. "Yes, always. That's the way I was brought up."

"Hmm." Her noncommittal response made him frown.

"I take it you didn't grow up attending church?"

She let out a harsh laugh. "Oh, sure. We attended church every week, but it didn't mean much. My parents only went to put on a show for everyone else. At home they argued and..." She didn't finish, but he felt himself grow tense.

"Your father abused your mother?" He was horrified by the thought and hoped Lacy hadn't been subjected to abuse, too.

She shrugged and avoided his gaze. "It wasn't like she had to go to the emergency room or anything, but yeah, he liked to hit. I have no idea why she put up with him."

He couldn't stop himself from reaching out to put a hand on her arm. "I'm sorry, Lacy. That should never happen."

She abruptly dropped her fork and jumped to her feet. "It wasn't as bad as what you're thinking. He didn't point a gun and shoot my mother in cold blood the way David murdered Jill."

Before he could say anything she disappeared into the tiny bathroom, closing the door behind her.

He felt terrible for opening old wounds, and gave himself a mental kick in the pants. Losing Carly had gutted him. Debra had torn his heart out and stomped on it, but even those two things were a far cry from what Lacy had experienced. Just because he needed some emotional distance from her and Rory didn't mean he couldn't be more sympathetic and understanding.

After promising himself to do better, he finished his meal and then cleaned up his things, leaving Lacy's meal alone. After about ten minutes she emerged from the bathroom, her red, puffy eyes evidence of her tears.

She didn't say anything to him, but took her seat and continued eating her breakfast.

"I'm sorry," he said gruffly. "I didn't mean to upset you."

She nodded and finished her meal. "I know," she said after she'd tossed out her garbage. "I'm fine. Now, tell me how we're going to approach your boss. I'm not convinced going into the police station is the right move."

He stared at her in amazement, wondering if she'd read his mind. "How did you know that's exactly what my plan was?" he said. "Rather than call, I think we should show up and go straight in to talk to my lieutenant, Bill Gray."

Her eyes narrowed. "I don't know Lieutenant Gray, so who's to say he'll believe me?"

"I was there when David aimed a gun at you," he reminded her. "And he cut Duchess, remember?"

"We assume he cut Duchess. We didn't actually see it," she corrected him. "Duchess could have cut herself on a fence trying to chase him."

He didn't like admitting she had a point. "My boss has faith in me. There's no reason for him not to believe you."

"Except for another police officer telling a completely different story," she said. "And he's had three years of lies about my sister to back him up."

"Listen, the forensic evidence at the crime scene will speak for itself. The truth will prevail above the lies. You don't have anything to worry about." He hesitated, then added, "I need you to trust me on this, okay?"

Her expression was full of agony, and he felt so bad he almost gave in. But what other option was there? They couldn't hide out here in a motel room indefinitely.

"Fine," she reluctantly agreed. "I hope your boss is as good as you say."

"He is." Matt glanced at his watch. They still had almost twenty minutes before they needed to leave. He wanted to stop for warm clothes and maybe a car seat, but the stores wouldn't open for a couple hours yet.

Lacy went over to pick up Rory and brought him to the bed. For a moment, the memory of Carly lying sick in a hospital bed flashed in his mind, and he pushed it away with an effort.

Nothing was going to happen to Rory. He wasn't sick. And Matt would do everything in his power to keep the little guy safe from harm.

He left Lacy alone and checked his cell phone for messages. Then, since there was internet access in the motel, he decided to search for the closest big-box store, where they could get everything they needed for Rory.

The closest one opened at nine o'clock, so he figured they could stop there after talking to his lieutenant. It was tempting to call ahead to the department, to make sure Bill Gray would be there, but he restrained himself.

When it was time to go, he went back to Lacy's room to help carry the baby's things. He noticed she'd made a bottle for him, ready for whenever he became hungry. If she was intimidated by caring for her young nephew, she wasn't showing it. He had to give her credit for thinking ahead.

When he had the baby stuff loaded in the car,

along with Duchess's food and water dishes, he went back inside. "Ready?"

Her expression was resigned, but she nodded. He opened the door and then escorted her to the SUV parked facing outward in the lot. Before she could get inside, the baby slipped down in the swaddling cloth. She'd bent over in an effort to hoist him back up when a loud gunshot rang through the air. He pushed Lacy down, horrified to see a round hole in the passenger-side window where Lacy's head had been seconds earlier.

"Get in!" He shoved her inside and slammed the door. He jumped into the driver's seat, determined to escape from the gunman.

More gunfire echoed, and Matt drove like a demolition derby driver, clenching his jaw, praying that the bullets wouldn't find their mark. He headed toward the route that happened to be closer to the trees, hoping to use them as cover.

Thankfully, his ploy worked. They'd gotten away, for now. But he couldn't rest or relax.

How on earth had Williams known where to find them?

FOUR

Her heart in her throat, Lacy clutched Rory close to her chest and silently prayed for God to keep them all safe. The gut-level instinct surprised her—she hadn't really thought much about God in the years after her parents had died.

But right here, right now, with the wind whistling through the small round bullet hole in the passenger-side window, proof that David Williams hadn't stopped searching for them, she wanted to believe that God was up there, watching over them.

That she, Matt and Rory weren't completely alone in this.

"Are you all right?" Matt asked in a hoarse voice.

"Y-yes." She and Rory weren't hurt. Scared senseless, but not physically injured.

"We need a new plan." Matt's tone was grim. "Williams is always one step ahead of us, and I don't like it. I can't figure out how he knew where to find us. Regardless, I'm not going to risk taking you anywhere near the police station."

The news should have been reassuring. She hadn't wanted to go to the authorities, afraid that even with Matt's support, his boss would lean toward believing David's version of events over hers. At the same time, being here alone with Matt didn't make her feel that much better. Oh, she trusted Matt, at least as far as his ability to keep her and Rory safe. But for how long?

Duchess woofed softly behind her. Okay, they weren't completely alone, but still. Eventually, they'd need help of the two-legged variety. Someone to provide backup. It wasn't as if traveling with a three-month-old and a K-9 was inconspicuous.

They were bound to attract attention.

"Thank you," she said softly.

"For what? Almost getting you killed?" His harsh tone didn't make her flinch because she knew he was upset with himself rather than with her.

"You saved us," she corrected him. "And I can't deny I'm glad we're not going to the police station."

He was silent for several long moments. "We need a place to go where we can hide off-grid for a while. I want to dig into Williams's background a bit."

The idea of hiding somewhere off-grid was appealing, but the thought of his investigating David made her blood run cold. "He's a sociopath," she said in a flat tone. "His entire world revolves around him. I'm not sure you'll ever figure out the logic behind all this."

His gaze met hers in the rearview mirror. "Try not to worry about it, okay? Duchess and I will protect you and Rory."

She attempted to smile. "I know. But can we please stop at a store to pick up a few things? Rory needs clothes, baby wipes and extra bottles. Not to mention a proper car seat."

He sighed. "Yeah, okay. But I'm going to drive to a store located on the opposite side of town, just in case. And once we have what you and Rory need, I'm going to call my brother Miles."

The news made her tense up all over again. "Are you sure it's safe? You said your brothers work in law enforcement. I highly doubt he'll be thrilled with the idea of us going into hiding rather than to the authorities."

Matt grinned. "You'd be surprised. Miles has done his share of breaking the rules. He'll be supportive of our plan, don't worry. Besides, I need a different vehicle and more cash."

Duchess pressed her nose against the back of Lacy's neck, making her smile. Between the K-9 officer and Matt's ever-present confidence, she was feeling better already. "All right. I'll trust your judgment."

Matt nodded and fell silent as they headed across town. The traffic wasn't too bad, and they reached a shopping area within thirty minutes. Lacy was relieved it was far away from the scene of her sister's murder.

She tightened her grip on Rory and blinked away the tears. Jill would want her to be strong for the baby, so she needed to stay focused on being a good mother. Once they were safe, there would be plenty of time to make sure Jill had a proper burial.

And hopefully by then David would be behind bars, paying for his crime.

"Ready?" Matt asked. He'd backed into a parking spot, and she belatedly realized he'd done that just in case they had to make a quick getaway.

"Yes." She unlatched the seat belt and curled her arm protectively around Rory as she pushed open the car door. Matt was there, offering his assistance. She put her hand in his, instantly aware of the warmth of his fingers curling over hers. As soon as she had her feet under her, she let go, uncomfortable about her odd awareness of him.

Matt was the complete opposite of the few men she'd tried dating in the past. One fellow teacher had expressed interest, but she hadn't experienced even the slightest flicker of attraction toward him.

Then there was the accountant who did her taxes, but that hadn't been any better.

So why was she reacting to a man who was virtually a stranger?

No clue. And it needed to stop right now.

The stern lecture to herself helped. They entered the store and Matt grabbed a shopping cart. She wove through the aisles, quickly finding the baby items she needed. A glimpse of the prices on the car seats made her grimace.

"They're so expensive." She glanced at Matt. "I only have about fifty dollars on me."

"It's fine, I have enough to last until my brother brings more. Which one do you think is the best?"

She looked at the various styles, then pointed at the one Jill had purchased. "This one."

"Okay." He picked up the box and set it in the cart. "Pick out everything you need for the baby, then we'll get you a light jacket."

She wanted to protest, but spring in Wisconsin was unpredictable so she gave in. She picked out two outfits for Rory, a warm zip-up onesie with a hood to cover his head and then a packet of baby wipes. The smallest box of bottles contained six, so she tossed that in the cart, too. Silently counting up what they owed made her stomach clench with worry.

"Women's clothes are over there," Matt said, turning the cart in that direction.

"I'll just get a heavy sweatshirt. No need to pay for a coat."

"You should get both, just in case." He apparently wasn't about to take no for an answer. And he didn't stop there. After she picked out a navy blue jacket, he pushed the cart over to the sundries and waved a hand. "Get what you need—hairbrush, shampoo, etcetera. I'll pick up a few things, too."

She hesitated. "If we're going to another motel, they'll provide some of this stuff. No reason to waste your money."

"We're not going to a motel," he countered. "It's too hard to find the ones that are dog-friendly, and they're not all willing to take cash, either. Besides, I want you and Rory far away from the area."

"So where are we going?"

"I have a friend who owns a cabin located about thirty minutes outside the city limits. It's nothing fancy, but it's warm, has two bedrooms and a kitchen. It's the best place I know where we can hide out for a while."

A cabin sounded nice, if maybe a little too cozy. And since the accommodations sounded better for Duchess, how could she argue? She began filling the cart with the bare essentials. Matt tossed a few items in, too.

The grand total was just as bad as she'd feared,

even though many of the items they'd purchased were on sale. She wondered how on earth she'd manage to repay Matt for his kindness.

Matt didn't seem concerned as he carried everything back out to the SUV. Right in the parking lot, he opened the box and quickly pulled out the infant car seat. Lacy bundled Rory into the new winter onesie and then fastened him into the car seat. Matt took over from there, securing the seat with ease.

"You look as if you've done that before," she said as she slid into the front passenger seat.

He froze for a moment, then shrugged. "A couple of my brothers have kids."

"A couple?" She fastened her seat belt then looked at him. "How many brothers do you have?"

"Four older brothers and a younger twin sister." He started the engine and let it run for a moment.

She tried not to gape at him. "Six? There are six of you?"

He pulled out his phone. "Yeah, crazy, huh? Marc is the oldest, and works for the FBI. He and his wife, Kari, are due to have another baby early next month. Miles is the second oldest and works as a homicide detective. He and his wife, Paige, are also expecting in early May. My twin, Maddy, just married my former partner, Noah Sinclair. Mitch, an arson investigator, and Mike, a private investigator, are still single, like me, which is good because we can balance things out."

All the information he was tossing out about his family made her head spin. And she hadn't missed the fact that he'd emphasized he was single and not interested in changing his status. Fine with her. "And you're sure they won't force you to take me in?"

"I'm sure." Matt reached over and lightly clasped her hand in his. "Trust me. In our family, Callahans always come first."

Strangely enough, she did trust him. As she listened to him leaving a message for Miles, she found herself relaxing for the first time since she'd woken up to the sounds of her sister arguing with her husband.

She reached back to place a soothing hand on Rory in his car seat. If Matt was right, and Callahans always came first, then maybe, just maybe, they'd find a way out of this mess.

Matt pulled out of the parking lot, hoping Miles would return his call soon. He didn't like thinking about the fact that as a cop, David Williams had access to information like Matt's cell number and his vehicle license plate number.

Five minutes later, his phone rang. He handed it to Lacy. "Place the call on speaker." When she'd done that, he quickly answered. "Miles, I need a hand."

"What's going on?"

"I need new disposable phones, a laptop computer, a new K-9 vehicle and cash."

"Anything else?" His brother's tone was all business. "What about a place to stay?"

"We need to remain off-grid, so I'm planning to head up to Valerie's father's cabin. Maybe you could give her a heads-up that I'll be staying there for a while, just in case she decides to take a trip."

"We?" Trust his brother to pick up on that slip.

He glanced at Lacy. "I'm keeping a woman and baby safe. There's already been three attempts to kill them. Honestly? The less you know, the better."

"Haven't I always supported you, Matt? I'm not about to turn you in, if that's what you're thinking."

Lacy relaxed in her seat, and he grinned. "I know that, and I trust you, bro. It's Lacy who's a bit skittish."

"Lacy obviously doesn't know us very well, does she?" Miles paused for a moment, then continued, "Okay, I'll meet you at Val's cabin in roughly forty-five minutes."

"Thanks, Miles. I owe you one."

"And don't think I won't collect. I think a night of babysitting should do the trick."

Babysitting? He grimaced but reluctantly agreed. "Sure, Abby is a cutie. But let's do that before the baby is born, okay? I'm not sure I can handle two of them at the same time."

His brother let out a bark of laughter. "Done. Catch up with you later."

"I guess the Callahans really do stick together," Lacy said, a hint of wistfulness in her eyes. "I'm glad."

He thought about the way she'd lost her sister and knew he'd never rest if someone had murdered one of his siblings. In fact, he'd been secretly trying to investigate his father's unsolved murder. Max Callahan had been the Milwaukee Chief of Police for almost five years before his death. He'd been shot when he'd gone out to visit the scene of a crime. Matt continued to be angry and upset that the perp was still at large.

But right now, he had to remain focused on keeping Lacy and Rory safe. He headed toward his college friend's cabin, using side streets and lesser known highways to avoid the interstate.

Because he'd taken the longer route, he reached the cabin a few minutes before Miles. Matt took a moment to make sure they could get inside, using the key that was hidden in the bottom of a bird feeder. The door creaked open. While it was a little dusty, the interior looked just the way he remembered. He returned to the SUV and let

Duchess out before carrying Rory's car seat inside, so the baby would have something to sit in. Lacy followed on his heels, bringing in the rest of their things. Duchess ran around for a bit, exploring the area before making her way back to the cabin. She barked, and he crossed over to let her in, taking a minute to check out her wound. Thankfully, it still looked good.

"Lacy, my brother Miles. Miles, this is Lacy and Rory."

"Nice to meet you," Miles said with a smile.

"You, too." Lacy shivered. "It's a bit chilly in here."

"I'll light the wood-burning stove. It will be warm in no time," Matt assured her.

Between the two men, they stacked armloads of cut wood near the vast iron stove. It didn't take long, and soon the logs were crackling and popping. He rose to his feet and turned toward his brother.

"Did you remember the computer?"

"Yep, it's in the SUV." Miles glanced at Lacy, who was busy unpacking their things. "Come outside for a moment."

Matt followed his brother outside. "What's up?"

"I'm sure you know about the Amber Alert. Lacy is wanted for kidnapping her nephew," Miles said. When Matt opened his mouth to protest, his brother waved a hand. "I told you I'd support you and I will. But I need to know what's going on."

Matt filled in the details, scant as they were. Miles scowled when he mentioned David Williams was a cop. "He's already tried to kill her three times. You'll find a bullet hole in my SUV to prove it."

They walked over to check out the damage, and Miles sighed heavily. "Okay, I trust you know what you're doing. The computer bag, cash and phones are in the front seat of the replacement SUV." His brother dangled the keys in front of him. Matt swapped with him. "Be careful, and let me know if you need backup."

"I will." Matt knew his brother probably didn't want to be too far from Paige, considering she was eight months pregnant, but he might need someone inside the police department to get him information. For any physical backup, he'd lean on either Mitch or Mike. "Thanks again."

"No problem." Miles slapped him on the back. "Lacy is pretty and the kid is cute, too."

Matt narrowed his gaze. "Just because you and Mark found the loves of your lives on a case doesn't mean I'm going to do the same. I'm finished with relationships, remember?"

"Yeah, we'll see." Miles grinned and slid in behind the wheel.

"Miles?" Matt put out a hand to stop him from closing the door. "Be careful, okay? Avoid taking the main highways. This vehicle has been targeted twice already. I need to know you'll be safe."

"I'll be fine."

Matt stepped back and watched for a moment as his brother drove away. He murmured a silent prayer for God to keep Miles safe before heading over to get the items Miles had brought for them. As soon as he had the computer up and running he wanted to start digging into David Williams's background.

When he entered the cabin, he heard high-pitched wails. Lacy was trying to get Rory to take his bottle, but the little guy wasn't having it.

A shiver of unease danced down his spine. "Is he okay?"

"I'm not sure." Lacy's expression reflected her concern. "I don't understand why he's suddenly so fussy."

He didn't know a lot about babies, but he'd heard that sometimes they cried because of gas pains. Maybe this was nothing more than that. "Here, let me try."

Lacy handed him the baby. He flipped the infant over his forearm so Rory was lying on his belly, and began rubbing his back in soothing circles.

The kid kept right on crying.

Matt tried walking around with him, putting an exaggerated bounce in his step. Duchess thought it was some sort of game and kept wrapping herself around his legs.

The kid continued to wail.

Was Rory missing his mother, instinctively knowing that he and Lacy were poor substitutes? Or was he just feeling colicky? He had no idea, but the incessant crying was making him feel a bit panicky.

"Here, I'll take him." Lacy extracted Rory from his arms, holding him protectively to her chest. There was a hint of fear in her eyes, and it took him a minute to figure out she was worried he was going to lose his temper over a crying baby.

"He'll likely cry himself out eventually. In the meantime, try changing him, then see if he'll eat," he advised calmly. "If not, we can take him for a car ride, see if that settles him down."

Lacy gave a tiny nod and hurried into the bedroom. The baby continued to cry, and when she returned five minutes later, she looked frazzled. "He still won't take the bottle. Let's try the car ride."

He closed the computer screen and nodded. He grabbed his jacket and gave his K-9 partner a hand signal that instantly brought the dog to his side. "Okay, let's go."

Lacy buckled Rory into his car seat, and he carried it outside and secured it in the back seat. He opened the back hatch for Duchess, then slid in behind the wheel.

"I hope nothing is seriously wrong. I don't even know the name of Rory's pediatrician," Lacy said in a low voice. "Maybe I should have purchased a thermometer. He feels a little warm, but maybe that's just because he's crying. I just don't know…"

"I'm sure he's fine." Matt did his best to infuse confidence in his tone.

Achoo! Achoo!

Rory's crying was interrupted by two consecutive sneezes. They would have been cute if they weren't so concerning. Matt didn't like thinking about how they'd been dragging this poor kid around the city, only just getting him something warm to wear a couple of hours ago.

He exchanged a worried glance with Lacy. What if the baby was indeed getting sick with some sort of flu virus?

No. Please, God, no. He couldn't bear the thought of something bad happening to Rory. He couldn't survive watching another innocent child struggle to breathe. To live.

Please, Lord, keep Rory safe in Your care!

FIVE

Lacy did her best to rein in her panic as she attempted to soothe Rory. So far, the car ride wasn't helping. She pulled out a tissue from the glove box and leaned back to wipe his face. The sound of his crying ripped at her heart.

The baby was so fussy, she knew something had to be wrong. This didn't seem like a simple case of colic, at least from what little she knew.

"Maybe we should take him to the emergency room." She looked at Matt. "I'd feel better if a doctor examined him."

Matt grimaced. "We can try, but without insurance information, they'll expect us to pay up front in cash."

Lacy had no idea how much an emergency department visit cost, but the fear of missing something serious with Rory outweighed her concern over money. "I still think it's worth it. What if he needs antibiotics? Babies are prone to inner ear infections, aren't they?"

"I think so," Matt agreed. "We'll take him in, but I'd rather go to a smaller hospital where we can be sure no one will recognize either of us, okay?" He hesitated, then added, "And we'll need to pretend to be married."

As much as she didn't like pretending to be something they weren't, she was relieved at the idea of Rory getting the help he needed. "Of course."

The baby's crying subsided to small hiccupping sobs that were no more reassuring than his loudest wails had been. His face was red and scrunched up, as if he were in so much distress that he couldn't stand it.

How did parents cope with the feeling of helplessness as they watched a sick child? A band of fear tightened around her chest. After everything Rory had been through, she couldn't bear the idea of his being ill. Although, maybe babies under stress were more likely to succumb to colds or ear infections.

She closed her eyes for a moment and sent up a silent prayer for God to watch over Rory.

"We're almost at the hospital," Matt said, drawing her attention from the baby. "We'll use my last name, if that's okay with you."

The thought of introducing herself as Lacy Callahan gave her a funny feeling in her stomach, but she nodded. Her name was linked to the

Amber Alert, and the last thing she wanted was for the ER staff to call the police on them. In fact, she decided to use her middle name of Marie.

Yes, Matt was the police, but so was David Williams. Returning Rory to his father was not an option.

Matt pulled into the small parking lot in front of the ER and took the first available slot. By the time she slid out of her seat, Rory had stopped crying.

"He's finally fallen asleep," Matt said in a hushed tone as they stood beside the open door, looking down at the infant car seat. "What do you think? Should we still go in or head back to the cabin?"

"I don't know," she whispered, agonizing over the decision. If they left and he began crying again, they could turn around and come back, but what if the delay in obtaining care caused him more harm? The alternative was to go inside and have the doctor examine him, which would undoubtedly wake him up. If there was nothing wrong, they would have wasted a big chunk of their spare cash for no good reason.

Rory's face was still red, probably from his crying jag, but the thought of the baby suffering from a fever swayed her decision.

"We're going in to be seen." She looked up

at Matt. "I won't be able to rest until I know for sure he's okay."

Matt nodded and, being careful not to jostle the sleeping baby, he unbuckled the car seat, lifting it out and then heading into the hospital's emergency entrance.

She closed the door quietly, then quickly followed them into the brightly lit building.

A nurse and registrar met them at the front desk. "Patient name and proof of insurance, please."

Fibbing didn't come natural to her, but for the sake of her nephew's health, she injected confidence into her tone as she used Rory's middle name. "Anthony Callahan, and unfortunately we don't have insurance. However, we do have money to pay our bill."

She held her breath as the registrar entered the information into her computer and then asked for a two hundred dollar deposit. Matt handed over the cash and they were led into the triage area, where a nurse began questioning them about Rory's symptoms.

"I believe he's running a fever, and I'm concerned he may have an ear infection," Lacy said. "I know we might be overreacting, but R—Anthony is such a good baby that this latest bout of crying and refusing to eat has me worried."

The nurse's smile was gentle. "I understand.

I'm going to get a quick set of vital signs, and then take a listen to his heart and lungs, okay?"

Lacy nodded and forced herself to step back as the nurse undressed Rory. He didn't like it and began to cry. She twisted her hands together, causing Matt to step up to put his arm reassuringly around her shoulders.

"He'll be fine," Matt said in a husky tone. She gave a terse nod but couldn't tear her gaze from Rory.

The nurse checked the baby from head to toe, listening with her stethoscope, although Lacy couldn't figure out what she would hear beyond his crying. She placed a device in Rory's ear that caused him to wail even louder.

"He is running a low-grade fever of 100.8," the nurse said. "He's acting like he may have an ear infection. The doctor will be able to tell for sure. Does your baby have any allergies?"

Allergies? She wracked her brain, trying to remember if Jill had ever mentioned anything like that. Lacy knew Rory had gone in for a two-month well-baby checkup, but had no idea if there had been other illnesses treated. "Not that I'm aware of."

The nurse nodded. "Okay, have a seat in the waiting room and we'll call you back when we have a doctor available to see your son."

She smiled, hoping the nurse couldn't tell it was forced. "Thank you."

Matt released her to step forward, lifting the car seat with ease.

They headed back to the waiting room, Rory's crying causing people to stare at them with obvious sympathy.

"I left his bottle in the car," she said as she unbuckled Rory from the carrier and lifted the baby in her arms. "Would you mind getting it for me? Maybe this time he really is hungry."

Matt nodded and headed outside. She stood and walked around with Rory propped against her shoulder, doing her best to soothe him. When Matt returned with the bottle, she took a seat and tried to coax Rory into taking it.

He latched onto the bottle, but after a few gulps began crying again. At least now it made sense— if Rory had an ear infection, his swallowing motion likely made the pain worse.

She set the bottle aside and lifted him back up against her shoulder. "It's okay, the doctor will give you some medication to make you all better."

"I hope so," Matt muttered. "I can't stand watching him suffer like this."

She wasn't so keen on it herself, but at least a simple ear infection wasn't anything to be alarmed about.

Twenty minutes later, they were taken back

into a room where a physician soon joined them. He performed a full exam, including looking into Rory's ears and throat.

"Anthony has the beginning of an ear infection on the right side," he finally said. "Looks like you caught it early, so that's good. We'll start him on an oral antibiotic, amoxicillin, twice a day for the next ten days. After he finishes the medication, take him into your regular pediatrician to make sure he's fully healed." The doctor wrote out a prescription and handed it to her. "Any questions?"

"Not that I can think of." She glanced at Matt, who also shook his head. "Thanks, Doctor."

"You're welcome." He left the room, no doubt moving onto his next patient. Ignoring the incessant crying as much as possible, she bundled Rory back into his one-piece fleece jacket and then placed him back in the infant carrier.

"Let's find a pharmacy," Matt said as they went outside to the SUV. Duchess lifted her head and thumped her tail in greeting. "The sooner he gets those antibiotics, the better."

"Sounds good to me." Lacy was exhausted from the lack of sleep she'd gotten the night before and now it appeared she wouldn't be getting much tonight, either.

The pharmacy was strategically located not far from the hospital, and within the hour they were on their way back to the cabin. Getting Rory to take the antibiotic was another challenge, but they finally managed it. Then she sat down in the old wooden rocking chair and tried once again to feed him. He took another few sips of his bottle, then fell asleep.

She gazed down at Rory's sleeping face, almost too exhausted to get up to lie him down in the dresser drawer she'd lined with a blanket to use in lieu of a crib. She felt Matt come up beside her.

"Would you like me to put him down?" he asked in a low husky voice.

"Yes, thank you," she whispered.

Matt slipped his large hands beneath the sleeping baby and gently lifted him up into his arms. He carried Rory into the room she was using as a bedroom, over to the drawer/crib, and set him down.

She followed Matt into the room, and for a moment it felt as if they really were Rory's parents, taking turns caring for him. Of course, nothing was further from the truth. Normally, she didn't trust men in general, yet here she was trusting Matt.

Not just to keep her and Rory safe, but also to help her provide care for Rory. Matt was so kind and so considerate, not losing his temper even when the baby cried inconsolably. Ridiculous fantasy, since she knew that once the danger was over she would be raising Rory on her own.

Still, long after she'd shut off the lamp and crawled into bed, she couldn't shake the notion that with Matt at her side, she wouldn't be nearly as afraid of what her future as Rory's mother would hold.

Matt woke up to sunlight streaming in through the cabin's living room window. He sat up on the sofa where he'd slept, looking around for Lacy. It was still early, seven thirty in the morning, but the silence was a bit unnerving. He noticed an empty bottle on the counter, and assumed Lacy and Rory must have been up at some point.

Taking a few minutes to load more wood into the stove, he smiled when Duchess rose from the rug she'd been lying on and went over to stand by the door. Dusting off his hands, he latched the woodstove shut. He quickly let the dog out, then padded into the kitchen, relieved to find a coffeemaker. Since his brother had been smart enough to buy coffee along with eggs and other essentials, he quickly brewed a pot. Once he let Duchess back inside and gave her food and water, he set about making breakfast.

Lacy joined him a few minutes later, looking adorably rumpled and sleepy. "I smell coffee."

He grinned. "That's always the first thing on

my morning agenda, too. Take a seat. I'll pour you a cup."

She seemed taken aback by his offer but dropped into the closest chair, her shoulders drooping with exhaustion. Duchess greeted Lacy with a sloppy kiss, tail wagging as Lacy scratched her behind the ears. He filled a large mug and brought over the milk, feeling guilty at having slept through Rory's crying.

"Did Rory keep you up a lot?" he asked.

She shrugged. "It's not his fault. Poor little guy finally fell soundly asleep around three in the morning. I'm sure he'll be up again any minute."

"Breakfast is just about ready. You eat, I'll take care of him when he wakes up." It was the least he could do, considering he'd been able to rest undisturbed.

She took a sip of her coffee and sighed with appreciation. "Boy, does that hit the spot."

"I remember you like scrambled eggs, so that's what I made. If you're tired of that, I can make them another way for you."

Her cheeks went pink. "Oh, please, don't bother. I'm not picky. I like eggs just about any way they can be made. No need to go out of your way on my account."

She acted as if no one had offered to do anything for her before, which was a concept he found disturbing. Granted, she'd witnessed her brother-in-law murder her sister, but surely there had been other men she'd had some exposure to? Men who didn't make a habit of hurting women?

He filled a plate full of scrambled eggs and set it on the table in front of her. "What's your favorite?"

"Favorite what?" Her blue eyes mirrored confusion.

"Breakfast food."

"Oh. I'm not picky, but if I had my top choice, I like French toast the best." She picked up the fork and dug into her meal. "Thanks, these are delicious."

"You're welcome." Her gratitude for basic things like a simple meal humbled him. But before he could ask anything further, he heard Rory begin to cry. "Finish your breakfast. I'll get him."

Hurrying into the bedroom, he found Rory squirming around in the blanket-lined drawer, arms and legs flailing. Duchess followed him and sat on her haunches, watching them. He lifted the little guy up in his arms, smelled the dirty diaper and sighed. Fine. He could handle this. Diapers and wipes were nearby so he changed the baby, the task taking twice as long as it should have. Rory stopped crying long enough to look up at him curiously with his wide blue eyes. Eyes that looked very much like Lacy's.

"Hey, big guy, I can tell you're much happier

now, aren't you?" Matt used to smirk at how his brothers had talked to their kids, yet now he completely understood. The baby's wide eyes held a level of understanding that surprised him. "Let's go find you something to eat, okay?"

Rory grinned a toothless smile. He bent over to press a kiss on the top of the baby's head, trying not to remember how he used to do that with Carly.

Duchess once again followed him and Rory into the kitchen, where he found Lacy making a fresh bottle. Her plate was empty and he couldn't help but ask, "Did you breathe between bites?"

She raised a brow at him over her shoulder. "Maybe, but to be honest, I don't remember."

"I told you I'd take care of him. I'm perfectly capable of feeding a baby." Matt crossed over to take the bottle, but Lacy shook her head.

"You haven't had breakfast."

"I won't starve," he said drily.

"That's not the point. I may as well practice doing everything myself, since I'll be raising Rory alone." She set the bottle on the counter and took the child from his arms, then picked it back up and went over to sit in the rocking chair.

In his opinion, Lacy's logic was flawed. She didn't have to do everything herself right now. There was no reason she couldn't ease into the transition of being a single mom. Although, he didn't like the idea of her raising Rory alone.

Not his business. He forced himself to shake off the strange sense of regret. Losing Carly had only proven how tenuous life really was, so he hardened his heart and turned back to the counter. After cracking more eggs into the bowl and whipping them with some milk, he made another batch of scrambled eggs, thinking about the next steps he needed to take in the investigation.

Rory's ear infection had distracted him from digging into David Williams's background. He was a cop, so if he could get into the police department database, he should be able to find the details he was looking for.

He booted up the computer, searching through information as he ate. Once his eggs were finished, he filled his coffee mug and accessed the MPD database.

Rory let out a loud burp, making him smile. He glanced over to where Lacy was caring for Rory. With the sunshine streaming in through the window, her blond hair was a sheen of pale gold. His heart tightened in his chest as he acknowledged once again just how beautiful she was.

Even more so when she was cooing over Rory.

He must have been staring longer than he'd realized because she abruptly looked at him. "Is something wrong?"

"Huh? Oh, no. Um, I was just wondering when he was due for his next dose of medication."

A hint of uncertainty shadowed her gaze. "I was thinking it would be good to get him on a more normal schedule, like nine in the morning and nine at night. But he had his last dose at one in the morning. Do you think it's too soon to give it to him again at nine?"

He lifted a shoulder in a shrug, feeling helpless. In his opinion, babies should come with some sort of instruction manual, but no one had asked him. "Maybe we should do it more gradually, like eleven in the morning and at night for today, then nine tomorrow."

She nodded. "You're right. That seems reasonable."

He turned his attention back to the computer. Unfortunately, the cabin Wi-Fi was much slower than he would have liked, and when he tried to log in to the police database, his access was denied.

Scowling at the computer, he tried again. The same error message flashed on the screen.

What in the world was going on? For a moment, he wondered if his access had been disconnected on purpose because he'd been suspended, or worse, fired. But wouldn't Miles have said something if that was the case?

He pulled out his new disposable phone and dialed his brother's number.

Miles answered after four rings, his voice thick with sleep. "Yeah?"

"It's Matt, did I wake you up?"

"Abby was sick in the middle of the night, so yeah, I was trying to sleep in." As he spoke, Miles started to sound more awake. "What's up?"

"Sorry to hear about Abby. If I had known, I would have waited till later."

"Forget about it. I'm up now."

"Okay, here's the issue. I'm locked out of the MPD database." Matt fought to keep his voice level. "Do I still have a job?"

"What? Of course you have a job. Why wouldn't you?"

"Then why can't I log in?"

"We only allow officers to log in from secure networks. The cabin must not be secure enough. Here, give me a minute to log in and I'll find what you need."

"Thanks, bro."

He heard rustling sounds before Miles came back on the line. "Okay, I'm logged in to the database. What do you need?"

"Everything you have on David Williams." Matt felt a little guilty about Miles digging into this under his own name, but hopefully it wouldn't matter once they'd arrested the guy for murdering his wife.

And for attempting to kill Lacy, Rory and Duchess.

"I can send this to you electronically if you would like, but was there something in particular you were interested in?" Miles asked.

"Lacy mentioned David had some sort of Special Forces training. What branch of the military was he in?"

"There's nothing listed here about any military service. Are you sure you have your facts straight?"

Matt turned in his seat. "Lacy? Why did you think David worked in the Special Forces?"

"Because he told me and Jill all about his—" she made air quotes with her fingers "—high-level military training. Why?"

Interesting. Matt spoke into the phone. "Send me the file, Miles, thanks."

He disconnected from the line and waited for the email from his brother to pop up on the screen.

David Williams had lied to his wife about his military service. But why? For what purpose? To scare and intimidate her?

And what else had he lied about?

SIX

Lacy rose to her feet, propped Rory on her hip and crossed over to the kitchen table. "What did you find out on David?"

Matt seemed to hesitate, then shrugged. "He lied about being in the military. There's nothing listed on his police application. The department does extensive background checks on potential candidates. It's not something he would have been able to pretend never happened or fudge."

She sat beside him, setting Rory on her lap so he could look around. "That's so strange. Why did he tell us he was in the Special Forces?"

"I have no idea. Although, you were the one who described him as a sociopath. Maybe he's a chronic liar, too." Matt's gaze zeroed in on the most recent email. "Give me a few minutes to go through the information my brother sent me."

Rory was squirming around again, so she wandered around the inside of the cabin, checking things out. She found an old radio and plugged it in to see if it worked.

To her surprise it did, although the reception was a bit fuzzy. Curious about the Amber Alert—after all, they wouldn't be able to hide out forever—she tuned in to a news station.

The reporter spoke about the recent stats on the murder rate in the city of Milwaukee, which was nothing new. Normally, she avoided the news. How much bad stuff could a person hear in one day? But she forced herself to continue listening, certain the outstanding Amber Alert would be mentioned.

But it wasn't.

She frowned. Why on earth would the Amber Alert be dropped? Or had the radio announcer already discussed it before she'd found the radio? Anything was possible.

"In other breaking news this morning, Judge Dugan has received two separate death threats in the past week. When questioned, Judge Dugan believes these threats are related to a recent case he presided over several months ago, involving Alexander Pietro. Because of the extensive criminal network Pietro has been involved with, Judge Dugan is requesting around-the-clock police protection."

"What did they say about Alexander Pietro?" Matt asked, his head snapping around to face her.

"Something about how the judge who presided over the case is getting death threats."

Matt abandoned his computer to come over to stand beside her. "My twin was the assistant district attorney assigned to that case, but the trial ended abruptly after the first day in a plea bargain. She almost died because of her determination to prosecute Alexander Pietro. But at the end of the day, she and my former partner, Noah Sinclair, managed to find the dirty cop who attempted to sabotage Pietro's trial."

Lacy wasn't sure where he was going with this information. "So that means what? That Judge Dugan shouldn't be getting death threats?"

He grimaced and jammed his fingers through his hair. "I don't know. It just seems odd that these death threats would come three months after the aborted trial. You would think they would have taken place before the trial, right?"

"I guess." She hated to admit she didn't care, since it obviously had nothing to do with David Williams. Unless— A horrible thought hit her. "Do you think David might have been another dirty cop involved in the crime? One that somehow managed to escape unscathed?"

He slowly shook his head. "I can't say for sure one way or the other, although I can give Noah a call to see if Williams's name popped up anywhere during the investigation."

The thought of a potential link between David Williams and another crime caused a flicker of hope to burn in her chest. This could be the answer to her prayers! If David's name was linked to a known criminal like this Pietro guy, then the police would have to believe her side of the story. How she'd listened while David shot her sister.

She returned to the rocking chair while Matt made the call to his former partner. She lifted Rory up so that he could stand on her lap, then bounced him up and down a bit, enjoying his laughter. The antibiotics must be working because he was already so much better than he'd been the night before. The doctor must have been right about how they'd caught the infection early.

So she'd done one thing right. Despite being plagued by self-doubt.

"Noah? It's Matt. How's Maddy?" Matt paused and then continued, "Glad to hear it. Hey, I have a question about the Pietro investigation. Did a cop by the name of David Williams come up at all?"

There was a long silence as Matt listened to whatever Noah was saying. She tried to stay focused on Rory, but every muscle in her body felt stretched to a breaking point.

David had to be involved. Maybe that was part of the reason he'd killed Jill. Maybe her sister had suspected something was going on, so David silenced her once and for all?

Although, that certainly wouldn't explain why he had threatened to kill Rory, too.

"Okay, thanks for checking." The disappointment in Matt's tone was clear, and her shoulders slumped in defeat. "Keep your ears open for anything related to David Williams, okay? I have reason to believe he's involved in murder."

Lacy told herself not to lose hope. David could still be involved. Maybe he'd just been good at covering his tracks.

"No links to the Pietro case," Matt told her, confirming what she'd already suspected. "But Noah will remain on alert, and so will Miles. If Williams is involved in anything else, we'll find out about it."

"Thanks, but I think we have to consider the fact that David's crime is solely centered on murdering my sister—why, I'm not sure, especially since he threatened to kill Rory, too." She couldn't hide her stark disappointment. "Now that we escaped, I wouldn't put it past him to stage the scene of the crime so it looks like I had something to do with Jill's death."

"Try not to worry," Matt urged. "I know I told you this before, but I firmly believe the truth will prevail."

Maybe he was right, but she couldn't help thinking that plenty of people got away with crimes every day. They weren't all brought to justice.

And the thought of David getting away with murdering her sister was too much to bear.

Needing distance, she abruptly shot to her feet, intending to head into the bedroom. But the front pocket of her hoodie got caught on the handle of the rocking chair, causing her to stumble.

Matt grabbed Rory as she struggled to stay upright. There was a tinkling sound as something metal hit the hardwood floor.

She stared in shocked surprise at the key that had fallen from her pocket. It took her a moment to remember how she'd accidentally stumbled upon the key in her haste to leave her sister's house the night of the murder.

"What is this for?" Matt asked, holding Rory close as he bent to retrieve the key.

"I have no idea." She reached over to take Rory, but the baby seemed to prefer being in Matt's arms. "I found it outside my sister's house the night I took off with Rory."

"You did? Is it possible Williams dropped it?"

"Maybe, but it's more likely to be Jill's, don't you think?"

Matt turned the key over with a frown. "It's too small to be a house key. In fact, it looks a little familiar."

"I don't know why I bothered to pick it up. Must have been pure instinct. All I could think about was getting Rory away from his father and keeping him safe." She shrugged, feeling guilty, as if she'd kept evidence from Matt on purpose. "I never gave the key another thought."

"That's okay. Better late than never." Matt slipped the key into the front pocket of his uniform pants. "I'll do some research on the computer, see if I can track down what kind of key it is."

Rory grabbed Matt's face and giggled. The baby clearly liked Matt, and for a moment her heart squeezed at the thought of Rory growing up without a father.

It wasn't as if she would be the only single mother in the world, though. Surely, those kids grew up to be well-adjusted adults. Having a two-parent household wasn't a requirement.

But watching Matt and Rory playing made her think about how much Rory would miss him once they went their separate ways.

The kid was too cute, and despite his need to protect his heart from caring too much, Matt found himself enchanted with Rory's antics. He sat on the edge of the sofa and gave Duchess the signal for Come.

The dog immediately came over, tail wagging. He instructed Duchess to sit. Rory reached out to pet Duchess's head, his movements clumsy.

Duchess was infinitely patient, stoically tolerating Rory's tiny hands batting at her.

"Easy, Rory. Be gentle, like this." Matt took Rory's little hand and lightly stroked Duchess's fur. The baby followed his lead for all of a moment before waving his arms around again.

"Duchess is a trooper," Lacy said, dropping down to sit beside him.

"Yeah, she's well-trained." Matt lifted Rory up over his head, and the baby laughed and laughed. "I can't get over how happy he is today."

"I know. It's a total change from last night." Lacy stroked Duchess. "It's a little scary how quickly a baby can get sick. If we hadn't taken him in right away…"

His gut tightened, and he brought Rory back down to his lap. He knew all about how fast kids could get sick.

How they could even die.

"Here, I need to take Duchess outside for a bit." With an abrupt motion, he plopped Rory on Lacy's lap and jumped to his feet. Duchess followed as he grabbed his jacket and headed outside.

K-9 officers needed ongoing training and reinforcement, so he took Duchess through the paces, more to keep his mind occupied than out of necessity. It wasn't easy to erase the memory of Carly's pale wan face, the way she'd looked just before she'd taken her last breath and passed into God's arms.

Knowing Carly was at peace should have made him feel better. But it hadn't.

For months, he'd found it difficult to pray, to understand God's plan. Eventually, he found some measure of solace in church services, but there were still times, like this, where the unfairness of it all came rushing back, nearly choking him.

He continued working with Duchess until he managed to get some semblance of control over his rioting emotions. Feeling better after exerting some physical exercise, he headed back inside.

After filling Duchess's water bowl, he poured himself another cup of coffee and sat back down behind the computer. The shape of the key niggled at the edges of his memory, but he couldn't for the life of him figure out where he'd seen something similar like it before.

Hopefully it would come to him, but in the meantime, he resumed reviewing Williams's file. The guy had a couple of reprimands for excessive force, but there was really nothing else of interest. Truthfully, he figured there were several cops that had worse records than what he'd found in this one.

He'd hoped, for Lacy's sake, that Williams might have been linked to the Pietro crime boss. He typed Judge Dugan's name in the search engine and discovered the article that had been mentioned by the radio newscaster.

The details were just as sketchy, so the article wasn't much help. It was dated yesterday, so basically old news.

Pulling the key out of his pocket, he peered at it again. The letter *W* was etched on the side, but that could mean anything. They lived in Wisconsin.

Searching different kinds of keys online gave him a little more information. The key Lacy had found was a typical pin-tumbler lock key. It wasn't a car key, but it was also smaller than a typical house key.

He sighed and shoved the key back into his pocket. It was frustrating to have a clue that didn't lead anywhere, although Lacy could be right— for all they knew, the key belonged to her sister rather than to Williams.

Maybe once they had an inkling of where to find the guy, the key would prove more useful. He went back to the file, staring intently at David Williams's official photograph.

Angular features, narrow eyes and jet black hair. According to the report, he was six feet three inches tall and weighed two hundred pounds. Going by his photograph, the guy wasn't fat, but appeared to be muscular, especially around the shoulders.

He frowned for a moment, flashing back to

the image of the guy wearing the black cap and taking aim at Lacy. His impression of the guy had been that he was lean rather than bulky with muscles. Also, the gunman hadn't appeared to be much taller than his own five feet eleven inches. Then again, Matt had only spared him a quick glance before rushing to protect Lacy, so he could have been wrong.

Or maybe, Williams had lost some weight since he'd initially joined the force.

Shaking off the sense of unease, he closed the file and sat back in his chair.

They weren't any further along on this case than they'd been on the night Lacy had escaped with Rory. He curled his fingers into fists, fighting back a wave of frustration.

There had to be something he was missing. Something he'd overlooked. He pulled out his phone and dialed Miles again.

"Now what?" Miles asked, a slight edge to his tone. "You do realize it's my day off."

No, he hadn't known that, but that would explain why Miles had been the one to get up with Abby. "I'm sorry, do you want to call me back at a better time?"

"No, it's fine. Ignore me. I'm just upset at Abby being sick and crabby from lack of sleep. What's up?"

"Do you have any idea which detective has been assigned to Jill Williams's murder?"

"Jill Williams?" Miles sounded confused. "I haven't heard much about it. When did it go down?"

Matt thought back. The night he'd rescued Lacy and Rory was late Monday night into early Tuesday morning. Today was Wednesday, but for some reason it seemed like they'd been hiding for weeks rather than a few days. "Monday night, same night the Amber Alert went out."

"It wasn't me, but I'll see what I can find out. Give me a couple of hours and I'll call you back."

"Thanks, Miles. I really appreciate it."

"No biggie. Later, bro." Miles disconnected from the call.

Matt didn't feel any better about his progress. Even knowing the name of the detective wouldn't help him much. It wasn't like he could call the guy up and ask for details related to the homicide investigation.

"Matt? Can you give me a hand with Rory?"

He swung around to face her, noticing she had the bottle of liquid antibiotic in her hand. Was it eleven o'clock already?

"Of course." He crossed over. "What do you need?"

"Hold him so I can get this syringe into his

mouth. He's squirming around and I don't want to waste any of the medication."

He took the wiggling baby and cradled him so that his head was nestled in the crook of his arm. He trapped Rory's arm against his body and then lightly grasped his other arm. Rory didn't like it and let out a wail.

"Come on, sweetie, you need to take your medicine." Lacy tucked the blunt end of the syringe in the corner of his mouth and gave him a little bit of the thick white stuff.

"Looks disgusting," Matt muttered.

She glared at him. "You're not helping. You don't want to go back to the ER, do you?"

"Yum, yum," he encouraged. "Come on, Rory, take your medicine like a man."

Lacy snorted but managed to encourage Rory to swallow more of the antibiotic. It seemed to take forever, and by the time they were finished, they were both feeling flustered.

"That was fun," Matt said with a wry smile. "Good thing we only need to do it twice a day."

"You're telling me," Lacy said, taking the syringe over to rinse it out in the sink. "When he started to spit some of it out, I panicked."

"I'm sure they factor some of that into their dosing," he assured her. Now that the medicine was in the baby's stomach where it belonged,

Rory was back to his usual cheerful self. "I feel bad that we didn't buy any baby toys for him."

"I have a rattle in my purse, but he's pretty tired of it." She dried her hands on a dish towel. "Who would have thought it would be such hard work entertaining a three-month-old?"

Not him, that was for sure. "Do you need me to hold him?"

"No thanks, I'm going to set him down on the floor for a while." She disappeared inside the bedroom, returning a few minutes later with the blanket they'd used to cushion the drawer that was doubling as a crib. "I think babies start to roll over at three months, don't they?"

Again, he had no clue. As much as he'd enjoyed spending time with Carly, much of that togetherness had taken place in the hospital where he'd held her during needle sticks or other painful tests and treatments. Plus, she'd been four, so the milestones of rolling and walking had long passed. Shying away from those memories, he focused on the present, setting Rory down in the middle of the blanket and placing the rattle out of reach, yet directly in his line of vision. Lacy sat on the floor watching him.

Rory bobbed his head up and down as if trying to move in order to get what he wanted. His little feet kicked out behind him as if he could propel himself forward.

When that didn't work, he arched his back. The motion caused him to roll over, and he looked about as surprised as he and Lacy were.

"Did you see that?" Lacy cried with excitement. "He's so smart."

It felt crazy to be ecstatic about a baby learning to roll over, but he couldn't deny feeling proud of the little guy. "Yeah, he sure is."

Lacy looked up at him, her smile lighting up her face, and for a moment he wanted nothing more than to kiss her.

Whoa, where did that come from? He abruptly stood and moved away, putting distance between them.

Kissing Lacy was not going to happen. He needed to remember that he was here to protect her, not to start something he had no intention of following through on.

No matter how beautiful she was.

He wished he could put even more space between them. The cabin was too small for his liking. He considered taking Duchess out again, but what he really wanted was physical activity to let off steam.

His gaze landed on the small pile of split logs sitting beside the woodstove. "I'm going outside to chop wood," he said. "Duchess, Guard."

Duchess plopped down beside Lacy and Rory, sitting with her head high and her ears perked forward. Smiling grimly, he headed out to find the ax.

It was propped near the woodpile, so he shed his jacket and began to chop wood. Within five minutes, he'd built up a sweat.

He paused and swiped a hand over his brow. This type of workout was just as good as heading to the gym after a long shift.

In fact, splitting logs might even be better than pumping iron.

An image suddenly flashed in his mind. Instantly, he remembered where he'd seen that key before!

Matt dropped the ax and dug into his pocket to look at the key. The *W* etched on the face clinched it. The Milwaukee Police Department provided a discount to all police officers to the Wisconsin Fitness Center. He personally used the facility on a regular basis, and there were several branches scattered around the city. Members could use a locker for free, or they could rent one and keep their stuff inside rather than hauling workout gear back and forth.

This key opened a gym locker!

SEVEN

Lacy's gaze strayed to watch Matt chopping wood, regardless of how hard she tried to remain focused on Rory. The baby was obviously feeling better, managing to entertain himself without her assistance.

Matt didn't need her attention, either, but he looked so athletically amazing, swinging the ax in a choreographed rhythm, that she couldn't seem to tear her gaze away. Normally, she wasn't impressed by a muscular guy, but watching as the force of the ax cut through the wood with a single blow, she felt a bit mesmerized by Matt's physical strength and ability.

In the past, physical strength in a man caused a sense of fear of that power being turned against her. But she didn't feel that way about Matt.

Instead, she was attracted to him.

Rory rolled over again, this time bumping into her knee. She glanced down in alarm. He didn't cry, but looked a little bemused, as if he didn't understand what had stopped him. She lifted him up, smiling at his wide toothless grin, then set him down in the middle of the blanket.

Once again, her gaze found Matt. He'd stopped chopping and was staring down at something in the palm of his hand. She frowned, wondering if he'd hurt himself. A blister, maybe?

He turned and strode purposefully toward the cabin. She leapt to her feet. Was there a first-aid kit? She hadn't seen one, but she also hadn't opened every single cupboard and drawer.

Matt burst in through the door.

"Are you bleeding?" she asked, crossing over to meet him. "I'll look for bandages."

"What? I'm not bleeding." Belatedly, she realized he had the key in his hand. "This belongs to a locker at the WFC. Wisconsin Fitness Center."

"Really? Which facility?"

He grimaced. "I'm not sure. Did your sister have a membership?"

"Not that I'm aware of, but Jill used to complain about how many hours David spent working out." She swallowed hard, trying not to dwell on the fact that she'd never see her sister again. "The key must be his."

Matt nodded. "Makes sense, although we can't necessarily rule out other gym members. WFC offers a discounted rate to the MPD." He turned the key over in his hand. "The key is marked with a *W* on one side and the number eighteen on the other. Eighteen could refer to a locker number."

"We should check the gym closest to my sister's house."

"Or the facility closest to the district Williams works out of," Matt said. "I tend to use the one closest to where I work."

Lacy crossed over to the laptop and opened a search engine. Before she could type in the name of the gym, Rory began to cry.

"Oh, no." She quickly rushed over to find he'd rolled off the blanket and was smooshed up against the leg of the end table, a red mark on his forehead. She scooped him into her arms, inwardly berating herself for being so inattentive. "I'm sorry, Rory," she murmured, pressing a kiss on the red mark. "It's okay, you're fine, I'm sorry…"

"What happened?" Matt came over, his green eyes shadowed with concern.

"I'm not a very good mother." She couldn't believe she'd even temporarily forgotten about Rory being on the floor. What if he'd hurt himself worse and needed stitches?

"Cut yourself a little slack, you've only been a mother for two days." Matt reached up and smoothed his hand over Rory's back. "Besides, I can't imagine he's the only baby who's ever rolled into something and bumped his head."

Logically, she knew he was right, but her pulse still raced with fear and worry. Obviously, she needed to make the cabin baby-proof. There were electrical outlets to worry about, and maybe other potential hazards she hadn't considered.

She battled back a wave of overwhelming helplessness. Lots of women raised a child on their own. She wasn't the type to shirk responsibility.

Yet any mistakes she made along the way could have serious consequences. It made her sick to think about inadvertently doing something to cause harm to an innocent baby. Rory had stopped crying for now, but what about next time?

"Lacy? Are you all right?" The tenderness in Matt's voice brought tears to her eyes.

She nodded, but kept her face hidden against Rory. Her throat was thick with emotion, making it impossible to speak.

Suddenly, Matt's arms came up around her, holding her and Rory close. His masculine scent was amazingly reassuring. "Shh, it's okay. I know God is guiding us on His path and that He'll keep Rory safe from harm."

Oddly enough, the idea of not being in this alone caused her tension to slip away. "I hope you're right, Matt. I'll need all the help I can get."

"You're going to be fine, Lacy. Just remember you're not alone," he said, his voice muffled against her hair. "God will always be there for you, and so will I."

She knew Matt had included himself just to be nice, because as soon as David was arrested, she and Rory wouldn't see him again. But right now, being held in his arms, she couldn't deny feeling stronger and more confident in her abilities. She thought it was related to Matt's influence, but maybe he'd been right to remind her about God. It never occurred to her to lean on God in times of trouble or distress.

Please, Lord, help me be a good mother to Rory.

A sense of peace filled her heart. She began to ease away from Matt's embrace, but he didn't seem inclined to let her go.

As much as she didn't want to leave, she sensed Rory had fallen asleep, and she needed to put him down for a nap. She placed her hand on Matt's chest and gently pushed. He dropped his arms and stepped back.

"Will you put the blanket back inside the drawer?" she asked in a hushed tone. "He's fallen asleep."

Matt nodded, swept the shawl wrap from the living room floor and lined the drawer/crib. When he finished, she gently set Rory down, hoping he wouldn't wake up.

Rory made a mewling sound and waved his

arms for a moment before falling back to sleep. She watched him, noticing the redness across his forehead was already beginning to fade.

She turned away and bumped into Matt. He captured her shoulders with his hands to steady her. He wasn't much taller than she was, their eyes almost level. She noticed his gaze lingering on her mouth and felt herself flush with awareness.

"Lacy." Her name was barely a whisper as he slowly drew her into his arms. He lowered his head, giving her plenty of time to stop him.

Ignoring the tiny voice in her mind that urged her to break away, she waited breathlessly for his kiss. His mouth lightly caressed hers, as if he didn't want to scare her.

She'd only kissed two men, and neither one of them came close to what she was experiencing with Matt. When he deepened their kiss, her legs wobbled, forcing her to cling to his shoulders.

This was everything a kiss should be.

But then Matt abruptly broke away from her, breathing heavy. "I have to get that," he said.

"What?" She had no idea what he was talking about.

"The phone. It's probably my brother." Matt turned and headed into the kitchen.

She dropped onto the edge of the bed and tried to pull herself together. No doubt the kiss they'd just shared had meant far more to her than it had to him. She hadn't even heard his phone, she'd been so caught up in the kiss. She needed to remember that men kissed women all the time. It didn't necessarily mean anything.

Except to her.

She told herself that Matt had only kissed her because she'd been upset over Rory's bump on the head. Being here in the cabin and hiding from David had created a false sense of intimacy. She was depending on him for safety, and he was depending on her to assist in testifying against her sister's murderer.

Losing her heart to Matthew Callahan wouldn't be smart. Rory was the priority here.

She'd gladly give up her personal life to provide a safe and stable upbringing for her nephew.

It was the least she could do.

Matt stumbled toward the kitchen, knocked seriously off balance by the sweetness of Lacy's kiss. He found the phone and quickly answered it. "Yeah?"

"What, did I interrupt your beauty sleep?" Miles asked in a dry tone.

Matt wasn't about to tell his brother that he'd interrupted an intense kiss. "No, I've been up for hours. Just finished chopping wood."

"That explains why you sound out of breath. Guess you're getting soft, huh?"

Matt wasn't in the mood for his older brother's teasing. Being the youngest of the four boys, not to mention the shortest, he was constantly trying to hold his own against their incessant banter.

"I'll take you on anytime, bro. Did you call for something important or just to hear yourself talk?"

Miles chuckled. "But you love hearing me talk. Actually, I just wanted to let you know that David Williams has gone AWOL and there's a warrant out for his arrest."

"He hasn't shown up for work? That's good news." Matt gathered his scattered thoughts. "When was the last time he was seen? Lacy thinks he's the one who issued the Amber Alert against her. I'm a little surprised he was able to deflect attention onto her."

"I haven't been able to get ahold of the police report from the night of Lacy's sister's murder," Miles said. "The homicide detective doesn't like me and is refusing to share any of the details, keeps insisting it's none of my business."

Technically, that was true, and Matt knew his brother well enough that if the situation were reversed, Miles wouldn't give out any information, either. "Thanks for the update. I found something else, too."

"What?" Miles sounded very interested.

"The night Lacy took off with her nephew, she found a key. I believe it belongs to a locker in one of the Wisconsin Fitness Centers."

Miles whistled. "Any idea which one?"

"Not yet, but I'm working on it." He trapped the phone between his shoulder and his ear, and typed the name of the gym in the search engine. "Which district does Williams work for?"

"The third district. I'm pretty sure there's a WFC nearby."

"Found it," Miles said, peering at the map that bloomed on the screen. "Five blocks south on Rochester Street. Although, there could be another one closer to where he lives."

"Hey, I have to go," Miles said abruptly. "A call just came in about a fresh homicide. So much for my day off. I'll check in with you later."

Matt absently disconnected from the line, zooming in on the fitness center closest to the third district police station. He didn't know Lacy's sister's address, so it was possible the key belonged to a locker at a different location, but he didn't think so. His gut told him that a guy like Williams would want to work out with his cop buddies, not a place closer to home.

Lacy came into the kitchen. "Are you hungry for lunch? I can throw together some soup and sandwiches."

"Sure, that would be great." He jotted down the address of the gym on Rochester, wondering when would be a good time to go. According to the website, the place was open 24/7, and he was certain it would be packed during the daytime.

But later, in the middle of the night? Might be easier to get inside to access the locker without a lot of curious eyes on him. Besides, he knew for a fact that a lot of cops used the gym either before or after their work shift.

Lacy brought over two bowls of soup and two turkey sandwiches. If she was angry at him for kissing her, she didn't show it. He reminded himself to stay on task. Lacy was a distraction he couldn't afford.

He closed the computer and smiled at her across the table before bowing his head to say grace. "Dear Lord, thank You for providing us with food and shelter, and please guide us as we continue to seek the truth. Amen."

"Amen," Lacy echoed.

He took a bite of his sandwich, wondering how she made a simple turkey and cheese sandwich taste so good. "Thanks, this is delicious."

"I'm glad."

He lightly tapped the computer. "I think my next step is to check out the gym locker. It's open all night, so I'll wait until you and Rory are asleep before heading out."

Her head snapped up. "What? You're leaving us here alone?" The sharp edge of her voice made him wince. "What if something happens? We won't have a vehicle to use if we need to escape. Are you taking Duchess, too?"

"Okay, you're right." He should have anticipated her reaction. "Leaving you alone isn't a good idea, with or without Duchess. I'll have one of my brothers come out for protection." If he could find one of them who wasn't too tied up in other cases. Miles was already a no-go, and he knew his oldest brother, Marc, was knee-deep in an FBI case. Mitch happened to be out of town for some arson training seminar, which only left Mike. He could potentially ask Noah for backup, but that would mean explaining Lacy to Maddy and he wasn't in the mood. As close as they were, she could be relentless when it came to questions about his personal life.

"I'd rather stick with you," Lacy said softly. "Rory may not be comfortable around a stranger."

She had a point, although in his opinion, the baby had adapted pretty well so far. Besides, if he left after they were asleep, Rory wouldn't even know a stranger was here. He pulled out his phone, determined to see if Mike was even available.

No answer. Possibly because Matt's call was coming in from an unknown phone number. He left a brief message, asking for a return call, then set the phone aside.

"What if he doesn't call back?" Lacy asked.

"I won't leave you here," he promised. "If Mike can't come, then we'll all go, okay?"

Lacy nodded, looking relieved.

He secretly hoped Mike wasn't also in the middle of a case. Working as a private investigator meant his brother set his own hours, yet it also meant that his paycheck was dependent on finishing his cases.

So what if Mike was busy? Matt didn't really believe that driving to a fitness center even late at night posed some sort of threat. Especially now that Miles had given him a different K-9 SUV. It wasn't likely that anyone would be able to find them.

Rory began to cry. Duchess lifted her head from the sofa, as if instinctively knowing the baby needed attention. Lacy jumped up and disappeared into the bedroom. While she changed and fed Rory, he cleaned up the lunch dishes, washing everything by hand.

He checked Duchess's incision, glad to see it still looked good, before they both went outside to walk the perimeter of the property. When he'd assured himself everything was fine, he stacked the wood he'd cut earlier into a neat pile. When

that was finished, he carried several logs inside
to stoke up the woodstove.

The rest of the afternoon dragged by slowly.
He wasn't used to being this inactive. It wasn't
until well after they'd finished eating dinner that
Mike returned his call.

"What's up?" his brother asked, getting straight
to the point. "I only have a few minutes."

His heart sank. "I could use some help later
tonight, if you aren't too busy."

"Unfortunately, I'm in the middle of something. Can it wait until tomorrow?"

Matt hesitated. "No, it's fine. Not a big deal.
But if anything changes, give me a call back,
okay?"

"Are you sure?" His brother's voice held in-
decision. "If it's important, I can bag my case."

"I'm positive. No need to drop everything. But
make a note of my new number okay? I'll call you
if things heat up."

"Sounds good. Talk to you later."

Matt felt the pressure of Lacy's curious gaze
so he forced a smile. "Mike is busy, but I'm not
worried. This is a low-risk endeavor. I'd like to
leave around one o'clock in the morning. It will
take roughly forty-five minutes to get there."

"All right," Lacy agreed.

"I can sit up with Rory for a while if you want
to take a nap," he offered.

"I'll lie down to get some rest after Rory takes his antibiotic at eleven o'clock." Lacy bounced Rory on her knee, but her blue eyes were serious. "Please don't leave without me, okay?"

"I won't," he assured her, remembering the panic on her face when he'd taken Duchess out for a walk at the motel.

An hour later, the cabin was quiet. Rory, Lacy and even Duchess had fallen asleep.

But Matt couldn't seem to relax. He dimmed the lights, stretched out on the sofa and closed his eyes, but his mind continued to race. He firmly believed David Williams would be arrested within the next day or so, and once the guy was behind bars, Lacy and Rory could return home.

Was that why he'd kissed her? Because he'd sensed their time together was coming to an end? And so what if it was? He wasn't interested in opening himself up to another relationship. And Lacy would have her hands full with caring for Rory, too.

This attraction they seemed to share couldn't go anywhere.

He must have dozed a bit because he woke abruptly at one in the morning, his internal alarm clock going off at just the right time. When he stood and headed into the bedroom to wake Lacy, Duchess followed, as if sensing the need to be back on guard duty.

It took almost twenty minutes for them to get on the road. Rory barely moved as Lacy tucked him in the car seat, and Matt hoped the little guy would sleep through the entire trip.

At exactly two o'clock, he pulled into the parking lot of the Wisconsin Fitness Center on Rochester Street. He backed the SUV into a space closest to the exit, more out of habit than because he expected trouble.

"Keep the car running and your phone handy," he advised. "I won't be long."

She nodded. "Okay."

He flashed a reassuring smile before sliding out from behind the wheel. Through the windows, he could see the place wasn't very busy. There were long rows of exercise equipment and maybe one older man walking on a treadmill.

Matt entered the building with confidence. Even though he'd never personally been to this location, his membership allowed him to go to any of the WFC gyms. He flashed his card at the woman behind the counter, then ducked into the men's locker room.

The place was empty. He took out the key and walked directly over to locker number eighteen. The key slid in and turned easily.

The smell of stinky clothes made him grimace, but it didn't deter him from his mission.

He pushed the clothing aside, hoping and praying this wasn't a wild goose chase.

At the bottom of the locker was a four by three inch spiral notebook. Curious, he pulled it out and flipped through it. There were letters and numbers listed, but at first glance it didn't make any sense.

He tucked the notebook beneath his arm and finished his search. The only item of interest was the notebook, so he quickly closed the locker and relocked it before heading out.

The woman behind the desk looked at him curiously, but he shrugged. "Gotta work," he said as an excuse, then ducked back out the front door.

He strode quickly to the SUV and climbed inside.

"What did you find?" she asked.

"This." He tossed the notebook in her lap, then clicked his seat belt into place. He put the car in gear just as a pair of headlights bloomed on the street, coming from the right-hand side.

Cars weren't completely unexpected at two o'clock in the morning, but still, he found himself going tense.

"Matt?" Lacy's voice was tentative. "What's going on?"

"Hang on," he said in a grim tone. He shot out of the parking space and instead of turning left, he turned right, directly facing the oncoming vehicle.

The headlights grew brighter, causing him to tighten his grip on the steering wheel. There was no doubt in his mind that the person driving the oncoming car was after the notebook. He'd walked into a trap.

"Matt?" Lacy's voice rose in panic. "Watch out!"

As the words left her mouth, the vehicle crossed the center line, heading straight toward them.

EIGHT

Lacy sucked in a harsh breath as the headlights grew large and bright and came straight for them. Bracing herself for the inevitable crash, she began to pray.

Dear Lord, protect us from harm!

Matt wrenched the steering wheel hard to the left in an attempt to avoid the oncoming car, narrowly missing a collision. Duchess scrambled for purchase in the back, as the SUV bumped wildly along the shoulder of the road. They were going the wrong way on the one-way street. At the next intersection, Matt turned left and then hit the gas hard to put distance between them and the vehicle that had tried to ram into them.

The headlights faded away behind them, but for how long? Had the driver gotten a good look at their license plate?

Lacy twisted in her seat, reaching out to make sure Rory was okay in his car seat. Amazingly, he was still sleeping. Duchess, too, appeared to be doing fine.

They were safe, at least for the moment.

Thank You, Lord!

"How did they know where to find us?" Lacy asked, breaking the strained silence.

Matt shook his head. "They must have had someone staked out at the gym. Although, to be honest, I'm not sure why they didn't just go inside and break into the locker themselves."

She thought about that. "They probably didn't know which locker belonged to David. I doubt the gym administrator would give out that type of information." The notebook had fallen to the floor in the chaos, so she bent forward and picked it up.

"They would in an official investigation," Matt said. "We know Williams is a cop. I'm sure his buddies would have been able to get the information they needed."

"Maybe they're not involved." She opened the notebook and squinted in the darkness, trying to read what was written inside. There were initials and numbers—was it some sort of code? "What does all this mean?"

"I don't know," Matt said slowly. "But my gut tells me Williams is likely involved in something illegal."

"More illegal than murder?" Lacy closed the notebook, thinking back to the night she'd been woken by the sound of voices arguing. Granted, she hadn't heard much, but there was no question that her sister had begged for her life and that Rory had been threatened seconds before the gunshot had echoed through the house.

From that moment on, everything was a blur. She still couldn't believe she'd managed to get Rory away unharmed.

"Is it possible your sister found out he was doing something illegal?" Matt asked, breaking into her thoughts.

She lifted her shoulders in a helpless shrug. "If so, she didn't mention it to me."

"But she did file for divorce."

Lacy shifted in her seat so she was partially facing him. "Yes. She was afraid of David, the way he seemed to get out of control when he was angry. Not only did he lash out at her, sometimes physically, but he was super controlling. He expected her to stay home every day, ready to answer his call no matter what she was doing. And if she did decide to go out, even to shop, he'd demand to know exactly what stores she'd gone to and who she'd talked to along the way. He'd often accused her of being a bad mother to Rory." She remembered Jill's tearfulness as her sister had finally told her everything that had been going on. "I hate that he started to hit her, the way our father lashed out at our mother. Jill didn't understand why David had turned so hateful. As if the man she'd married had ceased to exist."

Matt nodded thoughtfully. "Tell me again exactly what you overheard the night you escaped with Rory."

Lacy closed her eyes for a moment, trying to push past the painful memories. "They were arguing in low voices. I couldn't make out the words until David's voice got louder. He said, *Tell me the truth! Now! Or I'll kill you and the brat, too.*"

"The truth about what?" Matt asked.

"I assumed it was about her reason for the divorce. He never thought any of their problems were his fault. Or maybe he thought Jill was cheating on him." Although, now that she thought about it, the phrasing was a bit…off. "Since I couldn't hear the beginning of their argument, I can't say for sure what he wanted to know. But shortly afterward, Jill was begging for him to stop, pleading with him not to hurt her. I picked up Rory and called 911 to report the abuse, but right after I disconnected from the line, I heard two gunshots. I knew Rory would be his next target, so I ran."

Matt glanced at her, his expression serious. "I'm sorry. That must have been very difficult for you."

She swallowed hard, tearing up as the memories rushed back. It was all still so hard to believe. David had killed her sister without a moment's hesitation.

What kind of man could do something like that?

Immediately her father's harsh features flashed into her mind. Okay, maybe some men were just made that way. Yet, how was it that Jill had allowed herself to marry a guy who was so much like their father?

The night her parents had died in a car crash, the police had told them they believed their father had crashed into the side of the building on purpose, in a dual homicide/suicide attempt. Their rationale was that there had been no evidence of drugs or alcohol in their father's bloodstream and no sign that he'd even attempted to slam on the brakes.

The crash had killed both of them instantly. Leaving Lacy and Jill alone in the world at twenty-one and eighteen, respectively. Lacy had been able to finish her teaching degree, but Jill hadn't wanted to attend college. She'd met David at a mutual friend's party and married him a few years later.

Lacy had always suspected that Jill had been trying to replace the family they'd lost. A fact that had bothered her, because it wasn't as if they'd had a wonderful and happy childhood. What

Lacy remembered most was tiptoeing around the house when their father was home, everyone avoiding the possibility of making him mad.

"Lacy?" Matt sounded worried. "Are you okay?"

It wasn't easy to push her tumultuous past aside. Her parents were gone, and so was her sister. She needed to remain strong for Rory's sake.

She looked at Matt. "I just wish I would have convinced Jill to open up to me about her problems sooner. Maybe if I had, we could have gotten away from David before that night. Maybe Jill would be alive right now, caring for her son…"

"Lacy, this isn't your fault. Or your sister's fault." Matt reached over and took her hand, giving it a gentle squeeze. "Williams is the one responsible. And this notebook is actually proof that there is more to the story."

"David being involved in something illegal won't bring my sister back."

Matt continued to hold her hand. "I know. But we'll find him and arrest him. He'll pay for his crimes."

She wanted to believe Matt was right. But somehow, even the idea of having David locked up in jail where he belonged didn't make her feel better.

As if sensing her despair, Matt swept his thumb over the back of her hand, in a sweet reassuring caress. She stared at their joined hands, grappling with how much her life had changed in the past two days.

She was a mother now. Logically, she knew the full impact of that hadn't quite sunk into her brain. Having Rory fully dependent on her was scary. She was so afraid of failing.

Strange to think that a future with Rory could be any harder than being on the run from a crazy man determined to kill her and an innocent baby. The difference was, she had Matt to lean on, his strength and support to share the burden.

Of course, this dependency on Matt couldn't continue. Eventually, she would have to stand alone on her own two feet.

Her chest tightened with panic, but then she remembered last time, how Matt had taught her to lean on God in times of stress.

She wasn't completely alone. God would be there, guiding her.

The tightness eased in her chest as the realization sank deep. She'd be all right, as long as she had her faith.

Yet, she would miss Matt. He'd been a rock during this entire nightmare. And while he'd claimed that she could call him anytime, she knew she wouldn't.

Rory was her responsibility. It was up to her to provide Rory with a stable upbringing.

She would just have to find a way to survive without Matthew Callahan.

Matt drove in a circuitous route back to the cabin, unwilling to risk the possibility of being followed. Thankfully, at three in the morning, it was easy to make sure no one was on his tail.

It bothered him to think about how someone was watching the gym. He replayed in his mind the brief conversation Lacy had overheard the night of her sister's murder. He had the niggling suspicion that he was missing a key piece of the puzzle. It made more sense that Williams would want to silence his wife if she'd found out about his illegal activities. So what truth had he wanted to hear? And why would he stay at the scene of the murder to accuse Lacy and put out the Amber Alert?

Rory woke up crying as he pulled into the driveway at the cabin. He let Duchess out the back, then carried Rory's car seat inside.

Lacy unbuckled the baby and took the bottle she'd premade for him from her purse.

"Why don't you let me feed him?" Matt asked, noticing her weary expression. "I'm wide-awake anyway, but you look as if you could use some rest."

"Rory is my responsibility," she protested.

"And I'm here to help." Matt kept his tone firm.

"I won't be able to sleep, anyway. No reason for both of us to be up."

She wavered, then nodded. "All right. Thank you."

Matt cradled the baby in his arm and made himself comfortable in the rocking chair. Rory must have been hungry because he drank from the bottle with a single-minded intensity, his wide eyes glued to Matt's.

He tried not to compare Rory's glowing health to the emaciated way Carly had looked by the time she'd died. He'd loved that little girl, and his heart had broken in two when she had slipped away into God's arms. When Debra had announced she was reconciling with Kevin, the second blow had sent him to his knees.

He'd sought solace at church, trying to make sense out of God's plan. It took a while for him to accept that he might not ever understand what that plan may be. His job was to simply accept it.

God must have brought Lacy and Rory into his life for a reason. He'd been so determined not to let anyone get close to his heart again, but gazing down at Rory's innocent face, he realized he'd failed.

He cared about this little guy, far more than he should. Was this how his brothers had felt when they'd met their wives? Marc had met Kari when she had been pregnant, and even though their son,

Max, wasn't a Callahan by blood, he was an integral part of the family. And the same could be said for Abby. Miles's wife, Paige, had been a single mother to the six-year-old when he'd met her.

Both of their families were tied together by love rather than blood. And it occurred to him that love was the most powerful bond of all.

When Rory released his grip on the bottle, Matt carefully propped the baby up against his shoulder, rubbing his back the way he'd watched Lacy do. Rory's muffled burp made him smile.

The baby's eyelids began to droop. Rory took the last bit of his bottle and almost instantly fell asleep. Matt rose to his feet and silently padded into Lacy's room to set Rory into his makeshift crib.

He returned to the kitchen and began to examine the notebook. The initials likely represented people's names, and he soon realized there were dollar amounts attached to each one.

A blackmail scheme? Highly likely. But what was the source of the blackmail? Drugs? Gambling? Prostitutes?

There was no hint as to the source of the payments, either. The initials could have belonged to anyone—other cops, maybe, or politicians.

Matt set the notebook aside, turned off the lights and lay down on the sofa. Duchess came over to stretch out on the floor beside him.

He awoke to Rory's crying. With a groan, he forced himself upright, wishing for a solid four hours of sleep. He was about to get the baby, but when Rory quieted down, he knew Lacy had beaten him to it.

Duchess thumped her tail, got up and went over to the door, waiting patiently for him to join her. He took the dog outside, shivering in the cool brisk wind.

Another sweep of the perimeter reassured him their location hadn't been found. Satisfied for the moment, he waited for Duchess to finish her business, then headed back inside.

Lacy had Rory propped in his car seat as she made a fresh bottle. "Coffee is brewing. Should be ready soon."

"Okay." He glanced at his phone, wondering when Miles would call him back. Matt figured the police would apprehend David Williams sooner rather than later.

The police administrators wouldn't like the idea of a rogue cop running loose. They would want him behind bars as soon as possible. Matt figured every squad car on the streets was keeping a watchful eye out for him.

"Are you listening to me?"

He jerked around in guilty surprise. "No, sorry. I'm a bit distracted."

Her gaze was sympathetic. "I guess you didn't

get much sleep. I was just saying how great it is that Rory and I might be able to go home."

"I don't think it will be safe enough for you to head home," he said cautiously. He didn't like the thought of leaving Lacy and Rory vulnerable. "This notebook complicates things."

She frowned, shaking the bottle to disperse the formula. "You don't think the notebook is proof that David is involved in something illegal? With something solid to go on, wouldn't the police take the investigation from here?"

He could, but that would take the case out of his hands. He trusted his brothers and his brother-in-law, Noah, but everyone else? Not so much. "I'd like to understand what crimes the notebook is linked to before I do that."

Lacy picked up Rory from the car seat and sat down at the kitchen table to feed him. "I'm sure David will explain everything once he's arrested. Isn't that the way these things work? He gives the police information in exchange for a lighter sentence?"

"Sometimes," he agreed. "But he'd have to give up a lot of people in order to knock a few years off a murder charge."

Lacy grimaced and nodded. "You're probably right." She lightly stroked Rory's plump cheek. "I just hope David stays in jail long enough for me to raise Rory. The idea that he could get out early and insist on visitation rights…" She shivered.

"He won't get visitation rights," he assured her. "Especially when you testify to the fact that he threatened to kill him. No matter what happens, when this is over, you'll be able to raise Rory without Williams interfering."

He went over to get some coffee, then set about making breakfast. French toast was Lacy's favorite, so he went through all the cupboards until he found a bottle of maple syrup.

"French toast coming up," he announced.

She smiled with gratitude, and he found himself momentarily captivated by her beauty. Not just on the surface, although the wavy golden blond hair framing her oval face was certainly attractive. But there was a light radiating from her blue eyes that came from within, giving her a loveliness that was more than skin-deep.

He was so distracted, he nearly dropped the egg in his hand, managing to catch it before it hit the floor.

Focus, he reminded himself. He was here to keep her safe while figuring out why her brother-in-law wanted her dead.

When she'd finished feeding Rory, she once again spread the blanket out on the floor and set the baby down in the middle of it. Rory was a quick study and quickly began rolling over to get toward the rattle.

"You're so smart, aren't you?" Lacy picked him up again, moving him back to the center. He instantly rolled over, giggling at his new trick. "I wish your mommy was here to see this."

Matt tried to think of something to say that would make her feel better, but in the end he simply announced, "Breakfast is ready."

Lacy picked up Rory and set him back in his car seat. Duchess sat beside the baby, as if to watch over him.

He was surprised when Lacy led the mealtime prayer. "Dear Lord, we thank You for this food we are about to eat. We also thank You for watching over us last night and keeping us safe from danger. Please continue to guide us on Your chosen path. Amen."

"Amen," he echoed. "It's nice to hear you praying."

Her smile was shy. "It's nice to know God is always there for me."

He wanted nothing more than to lean over and kiss her. His phone rang, saving him from himself. He recognized his brother's number. "Hey, Miles, what's up?"

"I have some interesting news," Miles said. "Your case has officially intersected with mine."

Matt frowned. "What do you mean? How are you linked to Lacy's sister's murder?"

"Remember the call I took last night?" Miles asked. "I reported in at a murder scene. Adult male body had been dumped out in the middle of a stone quarry and was difficult to identify since the animals had gotten to him before we arrived."

An adult male? Matt's stomach clenched. "Did you get an ID on the victim?"

"Just now. Victim is none other than your missing cop, David Williams. The ME estimates he's been dead for at least twenty-four hours, maybe longer. We won't know more about the estimated time of death until the autopsy is completed."

"Williams is dead?" Matt echoed, his gaze locked on Lacy. She froze, her fork halfway to her mouth. "I get you don't know how long he's been out there, but what about cause of death?"

"Oh, yeah, forgot to mention that. Cause of death was a gunshot wound to the chest from close range. No gun found at the scene, either. No question it's a homicide."

Someone had killed David Williams. Who? And why? Either way, Matt was convinced the guy's death was linked to Jill's murder, or to the notebook he'd found in the gym locker.

Likely both.

He set the phone aside, his mind whirling. The

driver of the car that had tried to ram into them hadn't been Lacy's brother-in-law.

Which meant Lacy and Rory were still in danger, but from an unknown assailant.

NINE

The loud clank Lacy's fork made when she dropped it from nerves made Rory startle and cry. The little guy's distress was enough to pull her back together, and she quickly pushed away from the table to pick up the baby, cradling him close.

David Williams was dead. He'd never have a chance to hurt anyone else, especially Rory.

She closed her eyes for a moment, struggling between being grateful that the man she'd feared was gone for good, and despairing over the horrible way Rory had lost both of his parents.

Each one, a victim of murder.

"Lacy? Are you all right?"

She opened her eyes to find Matt standing beside her, concern darkening his green eyes. "I… guess. I can't deny I'm relieved to know the danger is over."

Matt's jaw clenched, and he momentarily glanced away before letting out a heavy sigh.

"I'm sorry, but the danger isn't over. Don't you remember how we barely escaped from the vehicle that had staked out the fitness center? Who was driving? Obviously not Williams."

A trickle of unease made her shiver. "But maybe the driver was only interested in the notebook you found, not in harming me or Rory."

Matt was shaking his head. "Listen, my brother seems to think that Williams has been dead for at least twenty-four hours, maybe longer. We won't know the exact timing of his murder until after the ME finishes the autopsy, but we have to consider the fact that someone else has been tracking us. Someone who thinks you know something important."

Rory had stopped crying and was wiggling around in her arms, so she placed him back down in the center of the blanket on the floor. Duchess came over as if offering her protection. "But I don't know anything."

"Are you sure? Maybe you need to think back to the day before Jill's murder. Could she have mentioned something that didn't seem important at the time?"

Rory rolled onto his back, kicking his feet and waving his arms. She watched him for a moment, trying to remember the conversations she'd shared with Jill.

Her sister had confided being afraid of David's

temper and filing for divorce. Jill had mentioned that David had punched holes in the wall of their bedroom and that he'd slapped her across the face in a moment of anger. Lacy remembered thinking it was a good thing Jill had taken that first step of filing for divorce, and she had encouraged her to obtain a restraining order against him, too.

Other than that, they'd mostly talked about Rory. Lacy had agreed to help with childcare duties whenever possible, and they'd worked out some scheduling issues.

Nothing that would cause somebody to come after her like this.

"Lacy? Let's finish our breakfast before it gets cold."

She wrinkled her nose, her appetite having disappeared, but followed him into the kitchen, anyway. She knew she needed to remain strong enough to care for Rory, so she ate a few more bites of her French toast.

Duchess let out a short bark, causing her to turn around in her seat.

"Hey, where are you going?" Matt jumped up from the table and rushed over to pick up Rory, who was trying to roll into the small stack of logs he'd brought in for the woodstove. Duchess had put her nose down in an attempt to stop him. "Good girl, Duchess. Rory, you're getting a little too good at rolling around. We need to find a way to keep you in one place."

Lacy swallowed the last bite of her breakfast and rose to her feet. "I can take him for a bit. Unless you'd rather I do the dishes?"

"No need, I can wash them." Matt handed her the baby, then returned to his meal. His appetite didn't seem to have suffered, she noted as he finished off the rest of his breakfast.

Bouncing Rory on her knee, she couldn't help but smile at how he laughed with glee. He was such a happy baby, at least now that he was taking antibiotics for his ear infection. Which reminded her, it was almost time for his morning dose.

"Matt, will you help me for a moment?"

"Sure." He didn't hesitate to come over. When he saw the bottle of liquid antibiotic in her hand, he grimaced. "Our favorite part of the day, huh, sport?"

Rory bobbed his head as if in agreement.

Lacy filled the oral syringe and waited for Matt to get a good grip on the baby. Rory still didn't seem to like the medicine, but most of it went into his tummy.

Mission accomplished.

She took the sofa cushions and used them to protect the perimeter of the blanket so Rory could roll around without her worrying about him getting hurt. Knowing the cabin wasn't exactly baby-proof made her wish she'd picked up a swing or some other baby items to help keep Rory occupied.

When Matt finished cleaning up in the kitchen, he refilled his coffee mug and returned to the kitchen table. Since Rory was content and well-protected, she walked over to add more coffee to her own mug, then joined him at the table.

"What's our next step?" she asked.

He shrugged. "I wish I knew."

She leaned in to take a closer look at the notebook. "Are those people's initials followed by dollar amounts?"

"That's my theory," Matt said.

"Blackmail," she whispered. "I wish I could say I'm surprised that David would become involved in something like this, but I'm not."

"Do you think your sister knew?"

She glanced at him in surprise. "Absolutely not. I'm sure if Jill had known, she would have told me and would have used it as leverage in the divorce."

"I suppose you're right," he agreed. "No reason not to use it against him."

"And no reason not to confide in me," she insisted. "I was already staying over on my school break to help out."

Matt's expression turned thoughtful. "When you found the locker key, did you have the impression it was dropped recently? Or is it possible it had been there for a while?"

"I have no clue. I guess if you're asking for a gut reaction, I believe it had been dropped recently." She thought back to the moment she'd slipped and had stopped herself from falling. Her hand had instantly felt the raised edges of the key. "It wasn't imbedded in the dirt the way it might have been if it had been lying around for a while."

"So David must have dropped it."

She lifted her shoulders. "Who else?"

He nodded and went back to paging through the notebook. She crossed over to the radio, tuning in to the same news station she'd listened to before.

"What are you doing?" Matt asked, his gaze curious.

"I'm wondering if the Amber Alert has been discontinued. It should be now that David has been found dead, right?"

"I would assume so," he agreed. He returned to the notebook as she listened to the news. The announcer seemed obsessed about Judge Dugan's death threats, since that was all he talked about.

Apparently judges ranked up there along with celebrities. Or maybe in a city as small as Milwaukee, political figures counted as celebrities.

After fifteen minutes, she shut the radio off and turned back to Matt.

Sensing her gaze, he pushed the notebook aside and gestured for her to take a seat beside him. He turned in his chair to face her. "Let's go at this from another angle. You mentioned that Jill didn't think anyone would believe her because Williams had friends on the force. Do you know who they were?"

"I can only remember Jill talking about two guys, Randal Whalen and Jeff Jones. But to be honest, there could be others. I had the sense he hung out with a group of guys."

"Those two are a good starting point." Matt pulled the computer closer and began a simple search. She was amazed at how quickly he found pictures of both cops. "Do either of these men look familiar?"

"Not really. I hate that I'm not being very helpful. I can't remember anything significant Jill might have told me, and I don't recognize these guys."

"Hey, it's all right." Matt must have heard the frustration in her voice because he reached out and took her hand. "You're a huge help—don't forget, if you hadn't picked up that key we wouldn't be on the right track."

Matt's hand was nice and warm around hers, and she wanted so badly to lean against him in an effort to absorb some of his strength. His fingers tightened around hers, causing her to blush. She hoped her thoughts weren't transparent.

He must have sensed her longing, because he slowly stood, pulling her up to her feet. Then he carefully cupped her face in his hand and leaned forward to capture her mouth in a gentle yet warm kiss.

In some tiny corner of her mind, she knew she shouldn't be kissing him like this. That her priority shouldn't be giving in to her deepest yearning to be held by a man who'd proven to be strong, yet gentle, caring and compassionate and, most of all, not the kind of man who would ever yell and hit.

"Waaah!"

Rory's shrill cry brought her crashing back to reality. She pulled out of Matt's embrace and hurried over to where Duchess was standing over the baby, as if determined to protect him.

"I'm here. Mommy's here." The word slipped from her mouth without conscious thought as she lifted the baby in her arms. He continued crying, and she propped him against her hip as she headed into the kitchen to make him a bottle.

"Let me help," Matt said in a low, gravelly voice.

She knew she needed to figure out how to do everything for Rory alone, but his crying grew louder, so she quickly nodded and handed him over to Matt.

She made Rory's bottle, mentally berating herself for not being better prepared. If she'd made several bottles ahead of time, she wouldn't have needed any help.

Then again, Rory could cry in his car seat as easily as he was crying in Matt's arms.

Shaking the formula in the bottle, she did her best to ignore the niggling panic. No more being distracted by Matt's kisses and warm embrace.

Rory needed her. Taking over as his mother was the least she could do for her sister.

She needed to remember that Rory was her single most important priority.

Matt reluctantly handed the baby over to Lacy, watching with admiration as she made herself comfortable in the rocking chair and began feeding him.

He forced himself to turn away, although it wasn't nearly as easy to push the memory of their kiss aside. Lacy was a bit like a skittish colt, coming close enough to hug and kiss him, but only briefly before running away.

Turning his attention to the two cops who were Williams's friends, Randal Whalen and Jeff Jones, he tried to find out more about their respective pasts. He found via social media they were both listed as single. Although searching deeper into the Milwaukee County case review, he discovered Whalen had divorced two years ago. There was no divorce on record for Jones.

That knowledge wasn't very helpful. He picked up his phone to call Miles.

"Yeah?" his brother answered. "Something wrong?"

"No, but I wanted you to know that Williams was close to a couple of guys on the job, Randal Whalen and Jeff Jones. Figured you might want to talk to them about when they last saw Williams."

"Thanks for the help, but I already got their names, in addition to a guy called Hugh Nichols."

Matt punched Nichols's name into the computer, bringing his picture up beside the other two officers. He looked vaguely familiar. "What else have you found out?"

His brother hesitated. "Matt, you know I'd help if I could, but I can't afford to compromise my case."

"You're the one who told me our cases are linked. Why wouldn't we share information?" Matt hesitated, then added, "I have some info that might be pertinent to Williams's murder."

"What?"

Matt pulled the notebook close. "The night Lacy's sister was murdered, she found a key outside. We figured out the key belonged to a locker at the Wisconsin Fitness Center, so we went over there last night."

"You found something in the locker? And you're just telling me now?" Miles's voice rose with indignation.

"I'm sorry, I should have mentioned it sooner, but hearing that Williams had been shot distracted me. Yes, we found a notebook. Looks as if your victim was involved in a blackmail scheme."

"What kind of blackmail?" Miles demanded.

"No idea. There's a list of initials followed by what appear to be dollar amounts. No other indication of what might be involved."

Miles was silent for a moment. "Okay, I'll head out to meet up with you shortly. I need that notebook."

"No way, Miles. I need it just as much as you do." Matt didn't like the idea of giving his brother the only clue they had. "Lacy and Rory are still in danger, and whoever is after them knows we have it."

"I'll figure out something. Maybe I can bring a portable scanner so that we can each have a copy. Give me a couple of hours. I'm still wading through evidence surrounding the crime scene."

"What kind of evidence?"

"Tire tracks near the edge of the quarry. Our theory is that the killer had Williams's body in the trunk and drove there to dispose of it. There isn't much blood at the scene, so the murder must have happened somewhere else. Also we found a small thread of fabric stuck to a prickly bush not far from the tire tracks, also possibly left behind by the killer."

"That isn't much," Matt said on a weary sigh.

"I know, but we're still going over things. There may be other clues, too. Oh, and I almost forgot to mention, Williams had last been seen three days ago."

Matt leapt to his feet. "Three days?" He counted backward from the night he'd witnessed the guy wearing the black cap pointing a gun at Lacy. Exactly three days ago. "You sure?"

"That's what we're hearing. Of course, these buddies of his could be lying, but he hadn't been at work for three days, either. The first two were normal days off, and the last day was when he was reported as AWOL."

"Okay, thanks, Miles. I appreciate you filling me in."

"You were right. We need to share information since our cases are linked. See you later."

"Bye." Matt disconnected and glanced over to where Lacy had Rory up against her shoulder, waiting for the infamous burp. The kid didn't disappoint.

"Sounds like you learned something new," Lacy said as she continued feeding Rory.

He nodded. "I'll give you the details when you're done."

While he waited, he took Duchess outside to let her run for a bit. His K-9 partner wasn't used to being cooped up inside for so long, and he felt guilty that he hadn't spent as much time training and working with her as he should have been. She ran as if she'd never been cut by the knife, and he was glad her wound was healing well.

He put her through a few commands, and she responded like a pro. Satisfied the incision hadn't interfered with her performance, he carried another armload of logs back inside.

Lacy was in the bedroom, no doubt putting Rory down for his nap. He stoked the woodstove, then went over to sit in front of the computer.

He didn't like the idea of Miles taking the notebook, but there was no denying it was linked to the guy's murder. He opened the notebook again, going down the list of initials. For the first time, he noticed that some were just two letters, such as R.B., and others were three letters, like J.L.J.

Middle names? Maybe. But why did some have middle initials and others didn't?

He caught the hint of lavender and looked up to see Lacy standing beside him. She had her arms crossed protectively across her chest, as if warning him not to try kissing her again.

"Have a seat and I'll tell you what I know."

She sat, making sure that there was a good foot of space between them. The way she held herself away from him stung, but he told himself to get over it. He filled her in on the tire tracks and thread that Miles had found at the quarry, along with the fact that Williams's coworkers claimed no one had seen him for three days.

"That doesn't make sense," she said with a frown. "David murdered Jill and then called his buddies to put out an Amber Alert. They must have seen him."

"Agreed, although it's odd they would lie about that since whoever had gone to the house that night would have called in Jill's murder, along with putting out the Amber Alert."

She lightly tapped the third face on the computer screen. "Who is this?"

"A guy by the name of Hugh Nichols, another of Williams's coworkers."

"Hugh Nichols, Jeff Jones and Randal Whalen," Lacy repeated softly. "I wish I'd paid more attention to what Jill told me about David's friends."

A series of initials caught his eye, three in a row.

H.N., J.L.J. and R.W.

His pulse jumped, and he stared in shock. The three cops he was close friends with? All in a row?

This couldn't possibly be a coincidence. For

one thing, he didn't believe in coincidences. Not when it came to linking clues to a murder.

A puzzle piece clicked into place. These guys weren't loyal to Williams because of friendship.

It made far more sense that they had been forced to support Williams because he had something to hold over their heads. Information to blackmail them with.

Certainly money, either from drugs, guns, prostitutes or gambling.

But which one? What was the blackmail scheme that Williams had been involved with that had ultimately resulted in his own demise?

TEN

Lacy leaned over to see what had captured Matt's attention in the notebook. It didn't take long for her to see the three initials listed one after the other and to understand the implication.

"He was blackmailing cops from his precinct?" she whispered in horror. "That's crazy."

Matt's expression was grim. "With what he was holding over their heads, it's likely they would have testified that you must have been the one to kill Jill in order to have Rory for yourself."

Her stomach twisted. "I'd never do something like that. Why would I? It's not as if being a single mother is glamorous. In fact, it's been downright scary having sole responsibility of a three-month-old baby."

"I'm not saying I believe it, just what they would have claimed. Although…" His voice trailed off. "It doesn't quite fit now that we know Williams was murdered."

She remembered listening to his part of the

conversation with Miles. "But they're still looking for clues, right? I'm sure they'll find something that will help."

"Yeah, maybe." Matt's voice lacked conviction. "Now that we know Williams's buddies are involved, I think I need to talk to my lieutenant, bring him up to speed on the latest developments in this case. Especially since we never showed up to report in."

Lacy understood Matt's concern about his job being on the line, but she really, *really* didn't want him to call his boss. Then again, she didn't want Miles to come and take possession of the notebook, either.

Since it wasn't possible to stay here in this cozy cabin forever, she forced herself to nod. "Okay, if you think that's what we need to do, then you should call your boss. Just…don't tell him where we are, okay?"

"I won't." Matt reached for his phone and began dialing.

She tried to ignore the sliver of apprehension by reaching over to scratch Duchess behind the ears. The K-9 officer made her long for a pet of her own. Maybe once Rory grew older, and she felt more competent caring for him.

Who was she kidding? It was doubtful she'd ever feel comfortable taking care of Rory by herself. Especially since she was bound to make mistakes along the way.

"Lieutenant Gray? This is Matthew Callahan. I have an update."

Matt's boss spoke so loudly she could hear everything without a problem. "Where have you been, Callahan? You were ordered to report in two days ago!"

"Yes, sir, but if you'd let me explain—"

"Explain what?" his boss interrupted harshly. "That you Callahans think the rules don't apply to you? That just because your old man was once the Chief of Police that you can do whatever you want? What part of 'an order is an order' do you not understand?"

"Sir, I picked up a tail that morning and the driver pulled a gun and tried to shoot us. I managed to lose him, but I wasn't about to risk bringing trouble to your office, so I found a place to hide out for a few days." Matt's voice was amazingly calm, as if he was used to getting yelled at.

She was tempted to pull the phone away so she could tell the lieutenant that Matt would never break the rules without a good reason. Somehow she knew this, even though she'd only known him a few days.

"Why didn't you call in before now?" Lieutenant Gray thundered. "Where are you?"

"I can't tell you that, sir. Not without putting

an innocent woman and baby in danger." Matt glanced at her and flashed a reassuring smile. "However, I can tell you that David Williams has been murdered. And I think I know why."

"Murdered? Let me guess, your brother was the one to give you that information?"

"Yes. Because David Williams's murder is linked to the murder of his wife, Jill Williams. I have proof that these cases intersect."

That made his lieutenant pause, and she couldn't hear him yelling anymore.

"The night of Jill's murder, Lacy found a key to a gym locker. We found a spiral notebook inside with initials followed by what appear to be dollar amounts. We believe that Williams was murdered because of his blackmail scheme."

Matt listened in silence for a few minutes, and she thought back to the night she'd overheard Jill's murder.

Tell me the truth! Now! Or I'll kill you and the brat, too.

A chill snaked down her spine. What if David wanted to know what Jill had learned about his blackmail scheme? Wasn't it possible that Jill had suspected something was going on? Say, for example, if someone had come to the house looking for David and alluded to the fact that he owed David money? Maybe while Lacy had been out at the park with Rory?

"Yes, sir. I'll report in tomorrow morning." Matt's voice brought her back to the present. "And I'll bring the notebook. My brother will likely join us."

Lacy wanted to cry out in protest. It was one thing to call his boss, but she didn't want to leave the cabin. It was the only place since this nightmare began that made her feel safe.

Of course, it wasn't the cabin itself, but staying in an isolated location with Matt and Duchess watching over them.

She glanced at the clock, noticing it was close to one o'clock in the afternoon. Seventeen hours at the most before they would be forced to leave.

Matt disconnected from the call and reached over to pat her arm. "We'll be okay, Lacy. You need to trust me on this."

She lifted her gaze to meet his. "I do trust you, Matt. But you're asking me to trust your boss, too. We already know that David's buddies were being blackmailed, and you have to admit there are likely others, too. Cops who would do anything to prevent the truth of whatever is indicated by that notebook from ever seeing the light of day."

"My boss isn't listed in the notebook," he assured her. "There are no B.G's or W.G's listed. And his middle name is Wayne, and there are no B.W.G's or W.W.G's, either. He's not involved in this."

"Still…" She was glad the lieutenant's initials weren't in the notebook, but that didn't mean they were in the clear.

"Besides," Matt continued, "we need to have faith in God's plan. He'll watch over us, Lacy."

She swallowed hard and tried to nod. Sure, she'd felt strong and calm when she'd prayed, but to blindly believe that God's plan included keeping her and Rory safe? They'd already been in danger several times since the night she'd listened to her sister beg for her life. God may have sent Matt and Duchess to the rescue, and she was grateful for that, but she was forced to admit that the danger wasn't over yet.

"Lacy?" Matt's husky voice saying her name caused a ripple of awareness to dance up her arm.

Battling a strong urge to throw herself into his arms, she abruptly stood, pulling away. "I need to check on Rory." Skirting around Duchess, she left the room, seeking the solace of the bedroom.

The baby was sleeping, his expression so peaceful and serene she felt tears well up, clouding her vision. She closed her eyes and dropped to her knees beside the drawer. She bowed her head and opened her heart.

Please, Lord. Please help me find a way to keep this innocent baby safe. I need You. Rory needs You, too. Please?

A sense of calm settled over her, and she slowly

rose to her feet. They only had what was left of today and tonight before they had to leave. Since it was past lunchtime, she decided to go and see what she could make that would tide them over until dinner.

When she returned to the kitchen, Matt was on the phone again. She made grilled cheese sandwiches, listening as he told his brother about Lieutenant Gray's insistence on reporting in and bringing the notebook.

There was a long silence as Matt listened to whatever his brother was saying. She could only imagine Miles wasn't happy with this latest news.

"Tell you what, Miles, bring a portable scanner," Matt suggested. "That way you can have the information, even if you don't have the actual notebook."

Another pause. "You found the gun?" Matt asked. "Where?"

She glanced over her shoulder, intrigued by the news. If they'd found the murder weapon, it was possible they were one step closer to making an arrest.

"Okay, we won't expect you until later, then. If you decide to meet up with us at Lieutenant Gray's office, that's fine, too. Whatever works." There was a brief silence, then Matt nodded. "Just call if you decide to come out to scan the notebook, okay? Bye, Miles."

Lacy finished making the grilled cheese just as Rory woke up from his nap. That kid sure did have a knack for knowing when she was about to eat.

"Sit down, I'll get him…" Matt started, but she quickly shook her head.

"No, thanks." She set a plate of food in front of Matt, then disappeared into the bedroom.

As she changed the baby, she thought about how soon she would be on her own caring for Rory.

"We're going to be all right," she whispered against his downy head. "I promise I'll do my best for you."

Rory smiled up at her with his wide toothless grin, and her heart filled with love.

Maybe Matt was right, and God would protect them. She needed to believe that in order to have the strength to move forward with whatever waited for them back in the city.

And if she missed Matt once this mess was over, she had no one to blame but herself. She'd become too dependent on him, and that had to stop—right now.

Before she lost her heart.

Matt wrestled with guilt as he stared at his sandwich. Why did he feel as if he'd betrayed Lacy by agreeing to meet with his boss?

He took a bite of his grilled cheese, glancing around the interior of the cabin. This place had been their temporary home for two days, nice and cozy in spite of the stressful circumstances.

But it was already clear that Rory needed his own room, a place to play. A house that had been baby-proofed with an actual crib and play area, something other than sofa cushions and Duchess watching over him.

Her sandwich was no doubt growing cold, and he wished there was a microwave to heat it up for her when she'd finished with Rory.

He assumed the reason she hadn't taken him up on his offer was because she was upset he'd called his boss. Still, it didn't make sense that she insisted on doing everything herself, because soon enough she really would be on her own.

The thought bothered him. A lot.

Lacy returned to the main area of the cabin with Rory propped on her hip. He scarfed down the rest of his sandwich and held out his arms. "My turn."

She hesitated, then shook her head. "No need. I'll set him down on the blanket for a bit."

He frowned but didn't argue. As much as he liked the little guy, he knew his focus needed to be on uncovering the details of the blackmail scheme.

The computer wasn't much help, so he turned

back to the notebook. Now that Miles had found the murder weapon, Matt knew his brother would likely be tied up for the next several hours, watching over the crime scene as a team of officers searched the rock quarry for shell casings.

Duchess rose to her feet and stretched. She headed over to where Rory was rolling around on the blanket, as if sensing it was part of her duty to watch over him.

Matt knew Duchess would do exactly that. Without hesitation. The same way he himself would.

Lacy joined him at the table and pried her cold sandwich apart.

"How about I make you a new one?" he offered.

She frowned. "No reason to waste food. Find anything interesting?"

"Not yet." He ran his finger down the list of numbers. "I can't even say for sure whether these figures represent tens or hundreds."

"Hundreds?" She looked horrified at the thought. "Surely not that much."

At this point, he wouldn't put anything past Williams, not even bilking hundreds of dollars from his fellow officers. But who else was on the list? Highly unlikely that it was all cops. Most of the officers he knew were good, law-abiding citizens. Business owners? Relatives of cops? Who else had Williams come into contact with?

Wait a minute—maybe he was looking at this all wrong. If this was blackmail for, say, either gambling or prostitution, then Williams must have known details. Which meant the guy somehow stumbled upon the illegal activity, and instead of arresting those involved, he had begun his blackmail operation.

A thrill of anticipation hummed in his blood. If he could figure out what cases Williams had been working on, he might find a hint of what the basis for the blackmail was about.

Matt made a mental note to ask his lieutenant for permission to review Williams's case files. When Lacy finished eating, he quickly went over to help clean up the dishes.

Lacy looked as if she was about to argue, but he shook his head. "Don't bother. We'll get this finished faster if we work together."

"Okay," she reluctantly agreed.

"I'm going to train Duchess for a while this afternoon," he said as he dried dishes. "Ongoing drills are important."

"Sounds good." Lacy's tone was polite, and he didn't quite understand why she was acting like they were nothing more than strangers, when in fact they'd kissed—not once, but twice.

Then it hit him. This was likely her way of

keeping distance between them, preventing him from holding her and kissing her again.

His heart squeezed painfully in his chest, but he ignored it. Wasn't that best for both of them? He wasn't interested in getting involved—with anyone, but especially someone who had a kid. A kid he could get too attached to.

They finished the chore in silence. When the last dish was put away, he hung up the towel and turned toward the living room.

"Duchess, Come."

His partner instantly rose and trotted over to sit right beside him, her spine straight, her tall brown ears perked forward as she waited for the next command. He pulled on his leather jacket and then opened the cabin door. Making a motion with his hand, he indicated that Duchess should accompany him outside.

The air was warming up, laden with the scent of spring. He put Duchess through the paces, rewarding her with toys and the occasional treat. Thankfully, his partner enjoyed training. Matt was exhausted and sweaty by the time they'd finished, but he also felt good about the way he and Duchess were able to connect and communicate with verbal commands or hand signals.

After four hours, he called it a day. Back inside the cabin, he found Lacy playing with Rory. She'd made a cloth doll out of rags and was using it to keep the baby occupied. He hung his coat on the hook by the door and checked his phone again.

Nothing yet from Miles, and he wondered if it wouldn't be better for his brother to just meet up with him in the morning.

The rest of the evening passed with excruciating slowness. Partially because he couldn't think of another angle to investigate, but mostly because of Lacy's aloofness.

The camaraderie they'd once shared had vanished as if it had never existed. Several times he found himself about to broach the subject but held back.

He didn't know what tomorrow would bring. It was entirely possible that the job of protecting Lacy and Rory would be handed off to someone else. He didn't like it, but that was the reality of working in law enforcement.

After a dinner of canned beef stew, Lacy fed Rory his bottle. When she finished, she turned toward him.

"I need your help to give Rory his antibiotic," she said in a low voice. "I just can't figure out how to do it by myself."

"I don't mind helping, Lacy." He gently took Rory from her arms, holding him so she could get him to take his medicine.

"Thanks." Lacy's smile was strained. "You seem to have a way with kids."

His gut clenched as he remembered caring for Carly. All the love in the world hadn't been enough to prevent the little girl from dying.

"I have some limited experience," he said. Confiding about his feelings wasn't easy, but he wanted to tell Lacy the truth. "I dated a woman who had a four-year-old, but things didn't work out."

"I'm sorry." Her expression was full of compassion. "That must have been rough."

"Yeah." He hesitated, then pushed on. "Carly had an aggressive form of leukemia and died. Afterward, Carly's mother dumped me to reunite with her ex-husband. I ended up losing them both in a matter of days and it was the hardest thing I've ever gone through."

Lacy's eyes widened. "Really?"

"Yes." He flashed a lopsided smile. "I don't talk about it much, but I wanted you to know we all have hidden issues in our past, they're nothing to be ashamed of. And I'm here if you ever want to talk."

She opened her mouth as if to say something, but then clamped her jaw shut and rose to her feet. The closed expression on her face wasn't reassuring.

"Hey." He put his hand on her arm to stop her. "I don't like it when you're upset with me."

"I'm not," she denied, avoiding his direct gaze.

"You are," he countered. "I'm sorry, I didn't intend to say things that would upset you."

Finally she looked at him. "You didn't, I appreciate your honesty. But you're right about the emotional turmoil related to the past. As you've figured out, I'm not good with trusting men. And I'm really not accustomed to being around someone like you."

"Like me?" he echoed in confusion.

"Nice and considerate and…" Her voice trailed off and she shook her head. "Never mind, I'm exhausted and not making much sense. If you don't mind, I'm going to head to bed early."

"Of course." He wanted to say more, to continue their conversation, but he let her go, sensing she'd already said more than she'd intended. Holding Rory in one arm, she picked up the blanket from the floor and disappeared into the bedroom.

Stretching out on the sofa, he bent his elbow behind his head and tried to relax. He felt better after telling her the truth about Debra and Carly, but wished she'd been as comfortable opening up to him. Maybe it would come over time. The idea that Lacy didn't know about nice men didn't sit well. She deserved so much better.

Duchess came over and curled up on the floor beside him. He hadn't expected to sleep, but must have because a soft noise woke him up.

He blinked in the darkness, trying to figure out what he'd heard. Lifting his head, he noticed Lacy was in the kitchen, pouring water into a kettle.

"Can't sleep?" he asked softly.

She spun around to face him, her hand hovering over her heart. "I'm sorry if I woke you."

"No biggie." He was about to sit up when Duchess abruptly leapt to her feet and ran over to the door. At first he assumed the dog had to go outside, but then she began to growl low in her throat.

Matt didn't waste a second. He shoved his feet into his shoes, then grabbed his weapon and his jacket. He picked up the phone, dialing Miles. "Go into the bedroom and watch over Rory," he commanded. "I'm calling my brother for backup."

"But that will take too long, won't it?" she protested as she turned off the burner beneath the tea kettle.

He didn't want to admit she was right. "Duchess and I are a team. We'll be fine. Stay in the bedroom and don't open the door to anyone except for me or one of my brothers."

"Be careful," Lacy whispered.

He nodded and called Miles. When he didn't answer, Matt tried Mike. Thankfully Mike picked up almost immediately. "What's wrong?"

Duchess's growling was getting louder, and Matt could only hope that whoever was outside would think twice about coming after them. "I need backup, ASAP."

"I'm already on my way, because Miles asked me to pick up some book," Mike said. "I'm armed. Hang on till I get there."

"I'll try." He slid the phone into his pocket. Pressing himself against the wall, he carefully opened the door.

Duchess was in full-alert mode, her nose practically twitching with the need to track the intruder. He exhaled and then darted outside, Duchess hot on his heels.

As they'd practiced earlier, he went left and Duchess went right. It took a few minutes for his eyes to adjust to the darkness. The new moon was barely a sliver in the sky, and there wasn't any snow on the ground to assist in picking out an intruder.

He made his way to the corner of the cabin, making sure no one was using the SUV for cover. Once he'd cleared that area, he paused to consider his next move. He heard Duchess moving through the brush and hoped she'd picked up the scent.

His partner let out a sharp bark, and he instinctively lunged toward the sound, his heart pounding with adrenaline. He moved from tree to tree. Suddenly a sharp crack echoed through the night, followed by a burning sensation along the outer edge of his left bicep.

He'd been shot!

Ignoring the pain, he continued his zigzagging path toward the area where Duchess had barked, alerting him to the presence of the gunman, silently praying that he and Duchess could hold the guy off long enough for Mike to arrive.

And to keep Lacy and Rory safe.

ELEVEN

Watching Matt and Duchess disappearing into the darkness outside gave Lacy an overwhelming sense of dread. Nausea swirled in her belly. She felt acutely vulnerable and alone, but forced herself to push aside her emotions in order to check on Rory.

The baby was sleeping. She watched him for a moment. Her instincts were to lift him up and wrap him against her body with the shawl, the way she had the night she'd escaped from Jill's. But doing that would risk waking him up, so she hesitated and considered her options.

What she needed was some sort of weapon.

She quickly returned to the main living space, sweeping her gaze over the area. A kitchen knife? She wrinkled her nose. The attacker would have to get close for it to be of use.

One of the split logs? Too bulky.

Fireplace poker? She picked it up, testing the

weight in her hand. Long enough to keep the intruder at arm's length, but not very heavy.

Since there wasn't anything better, she took the poker into the bedroom and stood protectively over Rory. Then she decided it would be best for Rory to be positioned well out of sight, so she slid the dresser drawer beneath the edge of the bed frame so he was completely protected, just in case whoever was lurking around outside managed to get past her.

Satisfied the baby was as safe as possible, she crossed over and stood near the doorway, her left side pressed against the wall, the fireplace poker resting on her right shoulder like a baseball bat.

Oppressive silence pressed against her chest, and every muscle in her body was tense. She silently prayed for strength and courage, hoping Matt was right and that God would watch over them. Especially an innocent baby like Rory.

A sense of calm nudged her fear aside. She would defend Rory, no matter what it took. No one would harm him, not while she was alive and kicking. If anyone but Matt or his brother came through the doorway, she would be ready.

The faint sound of Duchess barking reached her ears, causing her to hold her breath and listen carefully. Was that a good sign or a bad one? She didn't know, but hoped it meant Duchess had found the intruder's scent and was right now tracking him down.

A loud bang echoed through the night and she startled badly, gasping in horror. A gunshot? Was Matt the one shooting, or was it possible either he or Duchess had been the target?

And how had their location here at this remote cabin been found? The only call they'd made besides to Matt's brothers was to his boss.

Silence filled the cabin again, and she tried not to imagine Matt or Duchess lying on the ground bleeding. She swallowed hard, trying to decide what she should do. Matt had told her to stay here, but if he or Duchess were in trouble, shouldn't she take Rory and make a run for the SUV?

Or better yet, she needed to call 911 using the disposable phone. Matt said he'd called for backup, but she wasn't sure who would arrive first, the police or his brother. Being out in an isolated cabin didn't guarantee a quick emergency response. The shooter could easily break into the cabin before the police arrived.

That settled it. She had to do something.

Loosening her grip on the poker, she pulled the cell phone from her pocket and punched in the emergency number. Before she could push the send button, she heard the cabin door opening.

"Lacy, it's me, Matt. Are you and Rory all right?" Matt's voice caused a wave of relief to hit hard. She peeked around the corner, reassuring herself that he was really okay. He stood in the kitchen with Duchess at his side.

"I'm so glad to see you." She ran toward him, barely pausing long enough to toss the poker onto the sofa before throwing herself into his embrace. Matt wrapped his strong arms around her, holding her close. She closed her eyes for a moment, breathing in the aroma of pine trees mixed with his own unique scent and thanking God for keeping him safe.

"Hey, it's okay," he murmured, his face buried against her hair. "I'm fine and so is Duchess."

It took her a few minutes to find her voice. She didn't want to let him go but leaned back enough to look up into his eyes. "I heard the gunshot. Did you find him?"

"No, unfortunately he got away." The way Matt avoided her direct gaze made her frown.

"Did you get a good look at him?" she pressed. "Were you able to recognize him at all?"

"Not exactly." He dropped his arms and stepped away, and that's when she saw the dark wetness staining the side along his upper arm.

"You're hit!" Her voice came out in a squeak.

"It's nothing, just a scratch."

"Matt? Are you okay?" a voice called from outside.

"That's Mike." Matt opened the front door and

gestured for his brother to come in. "Thanks for getting here so quickly. I think the perp saw your headlights and knew I had help coming, so he took off."

The man who entered the cabin resembled Matt in some ways, but was a little taller with long dark hair that he wore loose around his face. Lacy crossed her arms over her chest, feeling ill at ease, even though she knew Matt's brother wasn't anyone to be afraid of.

Pathetic that she was only comfortable around Matt. Clearly, she needed to curb her dependence on the man.

But not tonight.

"Sit down so I can take a look at your injury," she said, addressing Matt.

"I'm fine. Now that Mike's here, we need to head back outside to check the area for clues. We can only hope the shooter left something behind."

Lacy wanted to protest, but Rory began to cry. Remembering she'd tucked his drawer beneath the bed, she dashed into the bedroom and gently pulled him out.

"It's okay, sweetie, I'm here. You're fine. We're all fine." It occurred to her that she was telling all this to Rory in an effort to soothe herself. She nuzzled his neck, changed his diaper and then brought him into the kitchen.

Matt, Mike and Duchess had all gone back outside, but this time, she wasn't afraid to be alone. Granted, the danger wasn't over, but she felt more secure knowing that Matt and Duchess had assistance. They would be okay.

She fed Rory his bottle, gazing down at his sweet face, her heart full of love.

This was what was important. Not her tangled feelings toward Matt, but caring for this little boy who'd already been through so much. She took a deep breath and let it out slowly.

She could do this. With God's help, anything was possible.

When Rory finished his bottle, she set him in the infant car seat and began washing bottles. She kept glancing at the clock, wondering what was taking the guys so long.

Had they found something?

It suddenly occurred to her that whether they had found a clue or not, this idyllic time at the cabin was over.

The wave of despair returned full force. Now that they'd been found, she was certain they would have to go back on the run once again.

"Over here," Matt called, when Duchess alerted near the base of a tree. The way she sniffed the ground, then sat down made him realize she'd discovered something. He crouched near the ground and carefully flashed a light over it.

Mike came over to join him. "What is it?"

Matt used his gloved hand to pick up the shell casing. "Belongs to a thirty-eight, standard issue weapon for cops. Proof the shooter was in this area when he took his shot at me."

"Okay, but where did he go from here?"

Matt glanced around and shrugged. "I'm not sure. But Duchess can help."

Mike nodded and stepped back, giving him room.

"Find, Duchess. Find!" He pointed to the ground where his partner had picked up the shooter's scent, and Duchess immediately went to work.

The dog sniffed around on the ground, then began following the scent, heading due south.

Matt trailed behind his partner, giving Duchess plenty of space to do what she was best at. Duchess was smart, but her path was anything but straight. In fact she wove in and around trees, often backtracking to alert on an area where the gunman's scent was particularly strong.

"Good girl," Matt praised. "Find, Duchess. Find!"

That was all the encouragement she needed to get back on track. On the third spot where Duchess alerted, Matt caught a glimpse of white. He went down on one knee and found what looked like a partial gum wrapper that still carried a hint of cinnamon.

It had definitely been left recently, but not necessarily by the gunman. Still, he picked it up with gloved fingers and placed it in an evidence bag with the same care he'd taken with the shell casing.

"What's that up ahead?" Mike asked.

Matt frowned and straightened. "I'm not sure. A road?"

"Duchess is heading straight for it," Mike pointed out.

Matt nodded and hurried to catch up with his partner. Duchess had indeed found what appeared to be a dirt road, with a fresh set of tire tracks.

Duchess alerted on the spot then picked something off the ground, bringing it over to Matt. He knelt down to take the item from his partner.

A black knit cap, just like the one he'd seen on the guy who'd shot at Lacy outside the gas station.

"Good girl," he praised.

"Nice," Mike agreed. "There may be a stray hair in there that we can use to match DNA."

Matt nodded, placing the hat in the evidence bag. Then he gestured to the ruts in the ground. "What kind of vehicle do you think was here? These look too small to belong to a truck."

Mike nodded. "I have to agree. They're barely

fourteen-inch tires. My best guess? They belong to a sedan of some sort."

"We can take pictures," Matt said thoughtfully. "It might be possible for someone in the forensic lab to find out more."

"You trust the forensic lab?" his brother asked drily. "I got the impression that you were pretty much working this case on your own, without support from the precinct."

That much was true, but then again, they would need this evidence to prosecute the case at some point. "Yeah, for now, but I'd still like you to take some photos."

"Fine with me." His brother went to work, taking photographs of the tire marks.

When Mike finished, Matt gestured toward the cabin. "Come on, let's head back. I don't feel comfortable leaving Lacy and Rory there alone any longer than necessary."

Mike quirked an eyebrow. "Really? Is that because of the potential danger, or because she's pretty and you're emotionally involved?"

He refused to take his brother's bait. "The danger is real. I have the wound, shell casing and hat to prove it. Come, Duchess," he commanded. His partner instantly came over, and he turned to head back toward the cabin. Thankfully, Mike left the subject of Lacy and Rory alone.

The interior warmth of the cabin greeted them.

Or maybe it was Lacy's tentative smile he was reacting to. He hadn't realized just how nice it was to have someone waiting when he walked in the door.

Man, he needed to get a grip. His brother was right—he shouldn't allow himself to become emotionally involved with the woman and baby he was duty-bound to protect.

"Did you find anything?" Lacy asked.

Matt nodded. "Yeah, the perp went through the woods until he came upon the dirt road where he must have left his car."

"Or where someone with a car was waiting for him," Mike added. "You don't know he was working alone."

"True." Matt shrugged out of his jacket, wincing as the movement aggravated his injury. "I need to wash up, then we'll have to hit the road. The cabin's been compromised."

"Yeah, any idea how this guy tracked you here?" Mike asked.

"It had to be the phone call Matt made to his boss," Lacy said, opening the small first-aid kit. "Sit down. I need to look at your arm."

"I'm fine," he protested.

"I'd rather decide for myself. The last thing I need is for you to get sick from some sort of infection."

He dropped into the chair but didn't dare

glance at Mike, afraid he would see the all-too-familiar knowing smile.

Lacy filled a bowl full of warm water and brought it over to the table. He shrugged out of his shirt, thankful he was wearing a T-shirt underneath. She leaned close, and he smelled a hint of baby shampoo mixed with lavender.

"This is more than a scratch," Lacy said sternly. "You should probably go to the ER. Antibiotic ointment may not be enough protection against a possible infection."

"I'm not going to the ER," he said, his tone sharper than he'd intended. "Just wrap it up for now. We can't afford to linger. The gunman could easily come back."

He could tell she wasn't happy, but she went about cleaning the wound, drying it and adding antibiotic ointment before wrapping gauze around his arm. He was acutely aware of the gentle touch of her fingertips against his skin and prayed she would hurry up already.

"Mike, don't you think he should go to the ER?" Lacy asked, stepping away, finally, to dispose of the bloodstained water in the sink.

"No, I don't." Matt shrugged back into his shirt, hiding a smile at his brother's blunt statement. "Gunshot wounds need to be reported to the police, and we don't have time for that nonsense."

Lacy scowled but didn't argue.

"Get your and Rory's things together, okay?" Matt caught Lacy's gaze and gave her a reassuring smile. "It will be fine."

Lacy nodded and disappeared into the bedroom. He opened cupboard doors, pulling out the food items they'd purchased along with the containers of formula. Mike helped, and it didn't take long to fill a couple of grocery bags.

"Guess there's no such thing as traveling light when it comes to a baby," his brother muttered.

"No, there isn't." He glanced down at Rory, who'd fallen back asleep after being fed. "For such a little guy, he needs a lot of stuff."

"I'll say." Mike hoisted the bags off the counter. "I think we should take my SUV into town. I'll get a ride back here to pick up this one. I don't like the idea that the gunman may have the license plate number."

Yeah, Matt didn't much like it, either. He took the last of the kitchen grocery bags, then slung the computer case over his shoulder, making sure the notebook was safely secured inside before following his brother out the door. Mike was in the process of securing Duchess's crate in the back of his SUV.

"Thanks for backing me up," Matt said, storing bags in the back seat.

Mike shrugged. "You'd do the same for me."

True. They walked silently back into the house,

and Matt noticed that Duchess was standing protectively over Rory's car seat. Lacy came out of the bedroom carrying three more grocery bags, her expression softening when she saw Duchess and Rory.

"She's so amazing," Lacy said in a low husky voice. "I had no idea what I was missing growing up. We never had pets. Jill and I always asked for one but our dad refused."

The thought of Lacy never owning a pet made him sad and angry at the same time. He truly didn't get people who didn't value pets. "You should get a dog, once this is over."

Her faint smile vanished. "Maybe. But I'm sure I'll be busy enough between working and taking care of Rory."

Matt almost offered his help, but Mike chose that moment to step between them, reaching for the bags Lacy held that contained diapers, clothing and a blanket.

"I'll take these to the car," his brother offered. "Bring Rory and whatever else Duchess needs. And don't forget to put out the fire in the woodstove."

Matt moved away to take care of the woodstove first, then tucked Duchess's food and water dishes beneath his arm. Lacy was holding on to Rory's car seat, the shawl wrapped around him to keep him warm.

"Ready?" he asked, taking the car seat from her fingers.

"I guess. Where are we going?"

"There's a hotel outside town that's run by a former firefighter and his brother. They're cop-friendly—in fact, the owner used to work with my brother Mitch."

"Okay." She preceded him outside.

He shut off the lights. "Come, Duchess," he said. He tucked Rory's car seat in the back, leaving Lacy to secure it with the seat belt so that he could get Duchess into the back. He slid in the front beside his brother, not liking the thought of leaving the police-issued SUV behind, but knowing it wasn't worth the risk.

Ten minutes later they were on the highway. Matt couldn't help stewing about how the phone call to his boss had been intercepted.

"We're not going in to meet your lieutenant, are we?" Lacy asked.

He and Mike exchanged a glance, and he knew they were both thinking about that thirty-eight shell casing they'd found.

"No," Matt assured her. "Not until I can figure out what's going on."

"Good." Lacy's relief was palpable as she relaxed into her seat and closed her eyes.

Matt filled his brother in on the events that had transpired over the past few days, including the contents of the notebook they'd found in Williams's gym locker.

"So it's highly likely the gunman really is a cop," Mike said in a hushed tone. They were being careful not to wake up Lacy and Rory.

"That's the way I'm leaning," Matt agreed.

"You trust your boss?" Mike asked.

He hesitated, then shrugged. "Right now, I don't trust anyone outside the family."

His brother nodded, and Matt knew he understood. The Callahan clan was known to stick together, through thick and thin. Yeah, they sometimes fought or argued, but at the end of the day, Matt would drop what he was doing to help any one of his siblings.

And they would do the same for him. But he couldn't stay off-grid indefinitely. He needed to figure out the blackmail scheme and who else was involved.

The gunman was either the person who had the most to lose if the truth came to light, or was hired by someone whose name was in that notebook.

He needed to uncover the truth, before it was too late.

TWELVE

Lacy awoke to the sound of muffled male voices. It took a moment for her to realize the car had stopped moving. She lifted her head, wincing at the crimp in her muscles from the odd angle at which she'd fallen asleep.

Gently massaging the back of her neck, she first checked to make sure Rory was okay, then squinted through the passenger-side window to where three men were standing outside, talking. Duchess was out there, too.

Matt and Mike were easy to recognize, but the third man took a moment to place. Oh, yes, Miles, the homicide detective.

The three Callahans were similar in size and build, but her gaze lingered on Matt, the most handsome, at least in her opinion. He wasn't as tall as the others, but there was something so compelling about him. More than just the fact that he'd kept her and Rory safe.

Enough mooning over the man. She gave herself a mental shake and averted her gaze to assess the motel. The American Lodge appeared to have two levels. Mike broke away from the group to walk inside the building, returning a few minutes later with what looked like small plastic key cards.

She pushed open her door and jumped out, shivering in the cool night air despite wearing the jacket Matt had purchased.

"Hi, Lacy. Here." Matt handed over one of the room keys. "We have connecting rooms just like last time, and they're both on the bottom floor, rooms two and three."

"Okay." She tucked the key in her coat pocket and turned to grab Rory's car seat. Before she could even open the door, Matt stopped her with a hand on her arm.

"Let me take care of hauling everything inside."

She hesitated, knowing that she needed to learn to do this stuff on her own, but was too exhausted to put up a fight.

Matt opened the door and carefully unbuckled the car seat without jostling the sleeping baby. She leaned in behind him to grab two of the plastic grocery bags, carrying them over to room three. The interior of the place was clean and tidy, a pleasant surprise. As an added bonus, there was both a crib and a small fridge tucked into the corner, perfect for storing Rory's bottles.

"Hope you'll be comfortable here," Matt said, brushing past her to set Rory's car seat in the center of the bed.

"It's great, thanks." She quickly began to unpack their belongings so that she would have everything ready before Rory woke up. It was late, just past midnight, and she had no idea how much longer he'd sleep.

Logically, it made sense to try to rest while he did, but she heard the brothers talking through the connecting door that Matt had left ajar, and she wanted to hear the plan.

After all, she was in danger, too.

"My hunch is gambling," Miles was saying as she entered. "These dollar amounts are likely related to high-stakes poker."

"Couldn't they be just as easily related to drugs or prostitution?" Matt asked. He took the notebook from his brother's fingers, glancing at her as she took a seat beside him. "We can't guess. We need to find out for sure."

For some odd reason, she didn't want Matt to give his brother the notebook. Not because she didn't trust Matt's family, but it was one of the only tangible pieces of evidence they'd found.

"May I?" she asked, tapping the notebook in Matt's hand.

He hesitated, then shrugged. "Why not? Miles will be taking it to the precinct soon."

She slowly turned the pages, searching for— what exactly? She'd already looked over the contents, going through the initials and numbers written alongside in small cramped script.

While flipping through the pages, she came across the halfway point, where the notations abruptly ended. The last initials were J.B.D.

She frowned, thinking they sounded familiar. But either she was imagining it, or was simply too exhausted to think clearly because she couldn't figure out why they would be.

There were, however, slight indentations on the opposite page, as if someone had written a note, pressing hard enough on the pad beneath to leave a mark.

She jumped to her feet. "I'll be right back."

"Lacy?" Matt called after her, but she ignored him. Moving silently in her room to avoid waking up Rory, she pulled out the small drawer beneath the desk. She immediately found what she was looking for—a dull, stubby pencil.

Matt came up to stand behind her, but she did her best to ignore him as she lightly brushed the lead tip over the page, revealing the markings that were left behind.

"Amazing," Matt whispered, his mouth close

enough to her ear that she could feel his warm breath caressing her skin.

"I think it's an address." She picked up the notebook and gestured for him to follow her back into the other room, where they wouldn't disturb Rory. "See? 2220 S. Handover Lane."

"You found an address?" Miles leapt up to meet them.

"I don't recognize it, do you?" Matt asked, showing him the address. He unpacked the laptop.

"Nope." Miles joined Matt as they peered at the computer screen, waiting for the internet to connect.

Lacy walked over to stand on Matt's other side, curious as to what sort of building the address belonged to. A private residence? Or some sort of business? She was glad to note that the address didn't match her sister's home.

It seemed to take forever for the computer to boot up and connect to the motel Wi-Fi. It wasn't secure, but since they were only looking at Google Maps, she hoped it didn't matter.

"Are you sure that's it?" Miles asked with a frown.

"This is what comes up when I type in the address," Matt confirmed. "It looks like some sort of nightclub called Secrets."

Miles grimaced. "Never heard of it."

"I have," Mike said. When his two brothers looked shocked, he held up his hands. "Hey, I only staked the place out. I never went inside."

Lacy leaned forward, trying to get a better view on the three-dimensional map. "It looks like a two-story building. Do you think they're both part of the nightclub?"

"Good question." Matt drummed his fingers on the table, glanced at the time and sighed. It was heading into one o'clock in the morning. "We need a copy of the blueprints."

"I bet Mitch could get them," Miles said. "But not until daylight hours. He came back to town yesterday from his conference."

"I'll give him a call first thing in the morning." Matt closed the laptop. "It's late. Why don't you guys head out to pick up my SUV at the cabin, and we'll touch base tomorrow."

"Okay," Miles agreed. "Although, I'm going to need to take the notebook in as evidence soon."

Lacy was tempted to pluck the notebook off the table and hold it protectively against her chest, but she needn't have worried. Matt didn't seem willing to let it go, either.

"Give me another twenty-four hours," he said. "Let's just see if we can figure out the source of the blackmail scam."

"Fine. But I'm going to take a few pictures of

the pages with my phone." He took out his cell and snapped several photographs.

"Mike, don't forget to email me the pictures of the tire tracks we found," Matt said as his brothers prepared to leave.

"Include me, too," Miles added.

Mike nodded, going outside with Miles, leaving a sudden quietness in their wake.

"That was good work, Lacy," Matt said, finally breaking the silence. "The nightclub is a great lead."

She flushed, touched by his praise. "I'm glad."

Matt took a step closer, then stopped. "You've been awesome through all of this. I'm sorry it's taking so long to get to the bottom of it."

"You've been trying, that's what counts." She told herself to turn around and get some rest before Rory woke up for his next feeding, but she wasn't ready to leave him.

She might not ever be ready to leave him.

The knowledge hit her with the force of a brick falling squarely on her head. Oh, no. No. She couldn't do this. She couldn't allow herself to start caring about Matthew Callahan.

"Excuse me, I need to get some sleep." She spun on her heel so fast she nearly fell over her own two feet. With as much grace as she could muster, she ducked into her room.

It was tempting to close and lock the connecting door, but what would that accomplish? Other than to let Matt know how rattled she was.

And prevent him from reaching them in an emergency.

Lacy pulled herself together and closed the connecting door so there was barely a sliver of light shining through. Then she turned and used the bathroom to brush her teeth before sliding into bed.

But as exhausted as she was, sleep didn't come easily. She kept thinking of Matt. Of what her life would be like without him.

About how much she would miss him.

After an hour of struggling with her emotions, she turned to God.

Please, Lord, give me the strength to walk away and to raise Rory on my own.

Matt forced himself to let Lacy go. Kissing her wasn't smart. She'd been traumatized by her past and so had he. This wasn't the time to dwell on their personal issues. He needed to stay focused on the case so that Lacy and Rory could get back to their normal everyday life.

He took Duchess outside for one last bathroom break, then stretched out on the bed. Duchess lay on the floor beside him. He slept in snatches, attuned to the slightest sound, anxious to get started investigating the nightclub. He felt certain that the place was the key to the information they needed.

The baby's crying brought him upright, and he wiped the sleep from his eyes and rose to his feet. Duchess thumped her tail, but didn't move. He padded through the connecting door. Lacy was still asleep, so he quickly picked Rory up from the crib and looked in the fridge for a bottle.

"Shh, it's okay. I've got you." He tucked the bottle beneath his arm and picked up the diaper and wipes before sneaking back into his room.

Lacy deserved a chance to sleep in. Changing dirty diapers wasn't at the top of his list of fun things to do, but he managed. After washing up, he began warming Rory's bottle under the hot water. Duchess languidly rose to her feet and stretched. She came over, sniffed the baby and licked Rory's cheek.

Rory didn't seem to mind. The baby smiled and played with his feet, then waved his arms around as if he might fly. Matt couldn't help but grin. He didn't have a lot of firsthand experience with babies. Sure, he'd given his brother Marc a hand on occasion, but he'd never taken care of Marc and Kari's son, Max, for more than a couple of hours.

Both Kari and Paige were due to deliver in the next few weeks, so the size of the Callahan family would be increasing very soon. Looking down at Rory, he could easily picture Lacy and Rory fitting right in.

Except he didn't do relationships. He wasn't interested in a ready-made family.

Was he?

Rory and Lacy were tempting, in more ways than one.

When Rory finished his bottle, Matt burped the baby and then held him up so the little guy could stand on his feet. Well, not stand exactly, but exercise his chubby legs.

Duchess went over to position herself by the door, signaling the need to go outside. He debated bundling up Rory and taking him out when he heard Lacy's voice.

"Matt?" She hovered uncertainly in the doorway between their rooms. "I'm sorry if he woke you."

"I don't mind," he responded. "Figured you could use the extra hour of sleep. And you have good timing. I need to take Duchess out."

Her expression turned troubled. "Okay. When you get back we need to give Rory another dose of antibiotic, too. But—did Rory cry? I mean, I can't believe I would sleep through that."

He didn't want her to feel guilty. Everything she'd been through the past few days was stressful enough. "He's a good baby. After I take Duchess out and give her some food and water, we can have breakfast. Are you hungry for anything in particular?"

She came in and lifted Rory from his arms. "I'll have whatever you're having."

"Sounds good." He resisted the urge to plant a kiss on both the baby's head and Lacy's cheek, instead he took Duchess outside while she did her business.

When he returned to the motel room, Lacy was playing with Rory. He dug in his pocket for the car keys Mike had left behind. "Give me a few minutes, okay? I'll leave Duchess here to keep an eye on things."

"All right." If Lacy was afraid to be alone, with only Duchess watching over her, she didn't show it.

It was well over an hour later by the time they'd finished eating and giving Rory his medicine. He called his brother Mitch, relieved when he picked up on the first ring.

"Hello?" his brother answered cautiously.

He realized Mitch hadn't recognized the number. "It's Matt. I need some help if you can spare it."

"Sure, what's up?"

"Are you familiar with a nightclub called Secrets?"

"Is this a test? Did Mom put you up to this?"

"No, it's related to a case I'm involved with."

The reference to their mother, Margaret Callahan, made him smile. Their mom lived with their grandmother, Nan, and the two of them would be upset if their sons decided to start frequenting the local nightclubs. "It's located at 2220 South Handover Lane."

"What kind of case?" Mitch asked. "Does it involve arson?"

"No, but I need a copy of the blueprints for the building. As an arson investigator, you have access to them, right?"

"Yeah, I can get them from the city," Mitch agreed. "When do you need them?"

"As soon as possible. We're staying at the American Lodge. If you could bring them over I'd appreciate it."

"We?" his brother echoed. "Who's we?"

"I'm protecting a woman named Lacy Germaine and her three-month-old nephew, Rory."

There was a pause as that information sank in. "Sure, why not? Good thing it's Friday. Otherwise, we would have to wait until after the weekend. Give me a couple of hours in case I have to cut through some red tape."

"You got it. Thanks, Mitch. I really appreciate it."

"I'll call you at this number when I'm on my way."

"Okay. Later." Matt disconnected, glancing

over to where Lacy stood with Rory perched on her hip. "It's all set. We'll have the blueprints in a couple of hours."

"Good." She tipped her head to the side. "I'm supposed to report in to work on Monday. Do you think we'll have this wrapped up by then?"

He hesitated, unwilling to gloss over the truth. "I don't know, Lacy. I can promise to do my best, but it all depends on what we find out about the blackmail scheme."

"I know. But since today is Friday, I'll need to let my principal know if I won't be there on Monday."

He walked toward her, wishing he could do something to make this situation better. "You would have to arrange day care for Rory before returning to work anyway, right?"

Her eyes widened and she went pale. "You're right. How could I be so stupid? Of course, I need to arrange child care."

"Hey, give yourself a break. Four days ago, you weren't solely responsible for Rory. Of course, there are a few things that you need to arrange. Will your principal give you time off?"

"I…guess he'll have to." She still looked a bit shell-shocked.

His heart ached for her. "Listen, I'm sure you deserve some bereavement time after your sister's death. And if he won't help you out, I'm sure my mother and grandmother wouldn't mind watching Rory for a couple of days."

Her face drained of color. "No! I mean, I couldn't possibly impose on them like that. They don't even know me."

"Hey, they've watched my brother's kids on occasion. I can guarantee they won't mind."

She swallowed hard, nodded and turned to go back to her room. He listened at the doorway as she called her principal to fill him in on her sister's murder and her need to take custody of her nephew. By the time she finished the conversation, she looked calmer. It seemed her boss had been understanding and had provided her the time off she needed.

Matt couldn't help feeling a little put off by the fact that she hadn't wanted his mother's and grandmother's help. Yeah, she'd mentioned several times that she needed to be independent, but there was no reason for her to turn her back on his offer.

His phone rang, and he absently answered it. "Hello?"

"Matt? I'm on my way, but there's a small problem," Mitch said.

"What kind of problem?"

"I've picked up a tail. Don't worry, I'll lose him, but it's going to take me longer than planned to meet up with you. Gotta go." Mitch abruptly disconnected.

Matt stood there for a moment, his mind reeling. How in the world had Mitch picked up a tail? His brother hadn't even gotten his phone number until an hour ago.

Was the shooter having every member of his family watched? It didn't seem possible. Then he thought back to the three officers whose names were in the notebook.

Three cops to keep an eye on his brothers, the ones most likely to give him a hand.

If that was the case, he shouldn't keep asking his brothers for help.

Once he had the blueprints, he would think of a way to work the case with Duchess as his only partner.

THIRTEEN

Principal Joel Harty had been understanding about her request for time off, even though it put him in a bind to find coverage for her at the last minute. Her teaching contract provided for bereavement leave, which took care of the first three days, and there was also a provision for adoption. If Jill didn't have a will it would take time for her to go through the formal adoption process.

Securing a couple of weeks off work should have made her feel better, but the reality of her situation was sobering. She needed to arrange day care, clean and put her sister's house up for sale, then find a new place to live. She didn't want to raise Rory in an apartment—besides, she only had one bedroom. And she also didn't want to live in Jill and David's house, not when her sister had been murdered there.

A wave of panic seized her by the throat, the enormity of the task ahead stealing her breath away. How on earth would she manage all of that in a couple weeks?

By taking it one step at a time and leaning on God's strength. Peace washed over her, wiping the panic away. She wasn't in this alone any longer. She had faith. And for now, she had Matthew Callahan. None of the arrangements she needed to make would matter until she and Rory were safe.

"Lacy? Are you all right?" Matt's voice mirrored his concern.

She smiled and nodded, shifting Rory to her other hip. "Sure. My boss granted me the time off. I don't need to report back to the classroom for three weeks. I can ask for another three weeks off, but it would be unpaid time. I figured I would hold off on that for now."

"Great. I'm happy to hear it."

She glanced around the motel room, realizing she'd been in her own little world for the past half hour. She hadn't paid the least bit of attention to Matt's side of the conversation. "So Mitch is bringing the nightclub blueprints?"

Matt's expression sobered. "Yeah, but there's a slight complication. He's picked up a tail. He needs to get rid of whoever is following him before heading over."

She dropped into the closest chair, her knees feeling weak. What next? First, being found at the cabin, and now this. It seemed like the gun-man was always one step ahead of them. "How? What does that mean?"

"I'm afraid that Williams's cop friends must have figured out I'd turn to my brothers for help, and they're attempting to keep an eye on them."

Lacy strove to remain calm, but it wasn't easy. She should be used to this type of thing by now. She thought about the fact that both Mike and Miles had come to their rescue. "Is it possible this motel is compromised? Do we need to move to a different location?"

"I don't think so. I know for a fact we weren't followed last night." Matt's gaze turned thought-ful. "But having a leak within the department isn't reassuring, either. They have access to a lot of resources. For all we know, there are other cops involved in the blackmail scheme. I can't stand the idea of placing my family in danger."

She shivered and cuddled Rory closer. "Okay then. We'll stay put for now. But we really need to understand what's going on. Why are they after us? Because of the notebook?"

Matt shrugged. "Probably. It shows a motive related to Williams's murder."

"Jill's murder, too," Lacy murmured. "I'm a witness, at least to what I overheard. But now that David is dead, it doesn't make sense that some guy is still coming after me."

"Keep in mind, you found the key to the locker," Matt pointed out. "It's possible he assumes you know more than you do. That you overheard information that might be used against them. Think about it—David kills your sister, then his buddies come out to help him. Only at some point, they kill him. Maybe Williams gave them some reason to believe you know all about the blackmail scheme."

Matt's theory was horrifying, yet logical. She swallowed hard. "All right, so they think I know details about the blackmail, and obviously, since you're helping me, they're assuming I've told you everything." Saying the words out loud didn't make them less terrifying. "What's to prevent them from assuming your brothers know everything as well?"

It was Matt's turn to drop into a chair. Duchess must have sensed his distress, because she came over and nudged him. He absently petted the dog. "You're right," he agreed, his voice low and gravelly. "It's too late. I've already put Mitch, Miles and Mike in danger."

"Hey, this isn't your fault." She edged her chair closer so she could rest her hand on his arm. "That's what you told me, remember? This is the gunman's fault, along with those cops who are trying to keep their little blackmail scheme a secret. They are the ones breaking the law.

The ones who placed your brothers in danger. Not you."

"I know." His tone lacked conviction. "I just— If something happens to them…" His voice trailed off and he shook his head helplessly.

"We need to keep our faith in God," she reminded him. "I hadn't really believed until you taught me about faith. Helped me to understand and to trust in God's plan."

After a long moment, he sighed, covered her hand with his and nodded. "You're right, Lacy. We needed someone to trust, and I would be there for any one of them."

"Of course you would." She was awestruck at how it must feel to have so many siblings, along with a mother and a grandmother, and hoped Matt knew how blessed he was.

Rory batted at her, and she looked at the baby, who happened to be the only family member she had left in the world.

Enough with the pity party. She disentangled her fingers from Matt's and rose to her feet. Rory was getting antsy, so she placed the blanket on the motel room floor and set him down. He immediately rolled over, giggling with joy. Then he planted his arms and lifted his head high, looking around at his surroundings.

"He's getting so strong," she said, amazed at

how quickly Rory was changing right before her eyes.

"Yeah, he sure is." Matt's phone rang and he quickly answered it. "Mitch? Everything okay?"

This time, she paid attention, keeping an eye on Rory so he wouldn't roll into the furniture. There wasn't nearly as much space here for him to move around as there had been at the cabin. She had to pick him up several times, placing him back in the center of the blanket.

"I'm glad to hear you lost him," Matt was saying. There was another long pause as he listened. "Okay, see you in fifteen."

Rory giggled again, obviously enjoying the game of rolling away from her. They played until there was a sharp knock at the door.

She picked Rory up off the floor and turned to meet yet another member of the Callahan clan. Like the other two brothers, Mitch was taller than Matt, but he had dark blond hair cut short. His eyes were bright blue compared to Matt's green ones. He had a long roll of papers tucked beneath his arm. He took a moment to bend over to rub Duchess before facing her and Matt.

"Thanks for coming. This is Lacy and her nephew, Rory."

Lacy stepped forward, offering her hand. "Nice to meet you."

"Likewise," Mitch said with a smile. "I'm sorry to hear you're in danger."

She nodded, glancing at Matt. "We're all in danger."

"We'll keep you and Rory safe," Matt assured her.

"I know." She held Matt's gaze for a long minute. He'd opened up to her about his past, but she hadn't been as good about telling him about herself. "I trust you more than I've ever trusted anyone in my entire life."

He took a step toward her, then abruptly stopped, as if remembering they weren't alone.

The air between them shimmered with awareness. For several long moments it was as if she and Matt were completely isolated in the room. She couldn't help thinking about their last kiss and wishing he would kiss her again.

Then Mitch seemed to notice the tension, too. "I'll—um—wait outside for a bit, give you guys some privacy."

"No need," Matt said, tearing his gaze away. "We have to focus on work."

That quickly, the moment was broken, leaving Lacy to wonder if Matt was fighting his feelings for her, or if it was nothing more than wishful thinking on her part. For all she knew, he wasn't ready for a relationship after the way he'd lost his former girlfriend and her daughter.

Which meant she was in big trouble.

Because she was certain her feelings for him were moving beyond the friendship category, morphing into something deeper.

"Thanks for getting the blueprints," Matt said, taking them from his brother and spreading them out on the bed. He needed to pull himself together. Thinking about how sweet it was to kiss Lacy wasn't smart.

In fact, one slip could get them all killed.

"What exactly are you looking for?" Mitch asked, staring down at the drawings.

He was keenly aware of Lacy leaving them alone, presumably to put Rory down in his crib. He reminded himself to focus on the case, not Lacy. "I'd like you to walk me through them first," Matt said. "I need to understand the layout of the place. This is the main floor, right?"

"Yes." Mitch pointed to the south side of the building. "This is the front door. The dance floor is here, and the bar area is along the east wall. There are a few offices here." He traced a finger over several small boxed-in shapes. "And an exit along the back of the building."

"Okay, what's on the second floor?"

"More club space, another dance floor and another bar."

Matt's shoulders slumped. He'd been so sure

this place was the key to figuring out what was going on. "I was hoping there would be private rooms of some kind."

"There's a large private room and a few smaller ones on the lower level." Mitch shuffled the blueprints around, pulling one from the bottom and laying it across the top. "Right here, see?"

"That's it," Matt said, satisfaction surging through his bloodstream. "I bet that's the location. Whatever they're doing down there would be drowned out by the loud music and dancing on the upper levels of the nightclub."

"Gambling?" Mitch suggested.

Matt nodded slowly. "Yeah, that's what Miles and I think. The notebook has initials with what look to be dollar amounts. There are other possibilities, but looking at the layout of the nightclub, I'm convinced they're running an illegal gambling ring."

"Why gambling?" Lacy asked from the connecting doorway, her pretty brow puckered in a frown.

"I think there are extra zeros that belong on the end of these dollar amounts. In other words, these are thousands, not hundreds. I can't imagine prostitution costing that much, or drugs for that matter." He dropped his gaze to the blueprint of the lower level of Secrets. "High-stakes gambling seems to fit the best."

Lacy approached the drawings. "And you think David found out about the gambling and was blackmailing the players?"

Matt hesitated, then shrugged. "This is all speculation at this point, but yes, let's say that he found out about the illegal gambling, maybe even played along for a while. But then he realized he could make more money by getting a cut of what the players won. So he began to blackmail them, threatening to go to the police commissioner with what he knew."

"But he was a cop, just as several of his buddies were cops," Lacy countered. "He couldn't possibly think he could blackmail them all."

"From what you described, Williams thought he was tough stuff. He claimed to be in the Special Forces, which wasn't true." Matt shrugged. "Maybe his buddies didn't figure out he was the one doing the blackmailing until recently."

"And that's when they killed him," Lacy agreed. "Except they didn't realize that David had hidden away his notes related to the people involved."

"Until we found it in his gym locker," Matt finished. "And only because you managed to find the key."

A faint smile tugged at the corner of Lacy's mouth. "Yeah, I guess I did."

Matt couldn't tear his gaze away from Lacy's.

How was it that he hadn't fully appreciated everything she'd contributed to the case so far? Without the notebook, they wouldn't even know about the blackmail.

"So what's the next move?" Mitch asked.

He turned toward his brother. "I think Duchess and I need to scope this place out, see if she can pick up the scent of the gunman."

Mitch looked perplexed. "How would she be able to do that?"

"One of the perps dropped his knit cap while escaping from the cabin." He pulled the evidence bag out of his pocket to show his brother. "We know the nightclub is tied to the blackmail. If we can connect the gunman to the nightclub, then we'll know for sure we're on the right track."

"Isn't it likely that the gunman is one of David's cop friends?" Lacy asked.

"Yes, but which one?"

"Maybe they're in it together," Mitch pointed out.

Matt hesitated, then shrugged. "I don't know, maybe. I saw one gunman attempt to kill Lacy outside the convenience store. And I think there was only one gunman outside the cabin. If he was working with someone, they would have attempted to flank the place in order to trap us. The more I think about it, the more I'm convinced we are hiding from one guy. A well-connected, talented cop who knows how to use his resources in tracking us down."

Mitch's cell phone shrilled loudly, drawing his attention to it. His brother turned away to answer it, and it didn't take long for Matt to realize that his brother was being called to the scene of a fire. "I'll be there in thirty minutes," Mitch promised, then faced him. "I'm sorry, but I have to go."

"I understand. Thanks for the blueprints." He walked Mitch to the door.

"Listen, be careful, okay?" Mitch said as he opened the motel room door. "Don't go into the club without backup."

"I won't," Matt assured him. "But I still need to do a little reconnaissance."

"Yeah, well, stay safe. I'll check in with you later." Mitch waved at Lacy before heading to his car.

"I hope you're not planning to leave me and Rory here alone," Lacy said, leveling him with a narrow glare.

"No, of course not." It would be one thing to leave Duchess behind to act as a guard, but he needed his partner's assistance in tracking the gunman's scent. "I guess we should wait for Rory to wake up."

"That would be nice," Lacy agreed. "And it won't take long for me to feed him first, either."

Matt used the time to work with Duchess for

a bit outside, then to study the blueprints Mitch had left behind. There was only one door leading down to the lower level from outside the building. There was another stairwell leading down from the offices located on the main level.

After Lacy had taken care of changing and feeding Rory, they headed out to the SUV. He put Duchess in the back, while Lacy buckled Rory into his car seat. Finally, they were on their way back into the city.

The nightclub wasn't difficult to find, although the building sure looked empty and vacant during the daytime. He was glad the place was closed down. It made it easier for Duchess to pick up the scent.

He drove past the building, then circled around to a spot located a couple of blocks away. "We're getting out here," he explained to Lacy. "I want you to drive around for a while, staying far away from here."

She gnawed at her lower lip. "For how long?"

"Twenty minutes. If Duchess can't pick up the gunman's scent by then, it's not likely she'll find it at all."

Lacy gave a tight nod. "Okay, so I'll meet you right here in twenty minutes."

"Yes. Keep your phone handy, just in case." He shut the engine down and handed her the keys. Then he released the back hatch, letting Duchess out. "If something happens, call one of my brothers," he added, as he slid out from behind the wheel. "Start with Miles, then Mike, then Mitch."

Lacy switched places, climbing over the console to the driver's seat. "Matt?"

He glanced over his shoulder. "Yes?"

She pressed her lips together, then tried to smile. "Be careful, okay? I expect to see you here in twenty minutes."

"Will do." He shut the car door and waited for her to pull away before turning his attention to his partner. "Come, Duchess."

The dog came to stand beside him and he walked toward the nightclub, scanning the area for anything suspicious.

A block from the building, he stopped and offered the scent in the evidence bag to Duchess. "Find, Duchess. Find!"

Duchess buried her nose in the knit cap, then went to work. She sniffed the ground, weaving back and forth as she attempted to pick up the scent. The conditions weren't ideal—finding a scent in nature was easier than in the city—but he hoped, prayed, Duchess would come through for him.

She alerted on a spot where a grassy area met up against the sidewalk. "Good girl," he praised, rubbing her glossy coat. "Find, Duchess."

Duchess continued tracking the scent, leading

him to the back door of the building, the one that would take people down to the lower level and the private rooms there.

"Good girl, Duchess." Now he knew for certain the gunman had been here.

Glancing at his watch, he realized that he only had six minutes to get back to the meeting spot. He put Duchess on the leash and left the nightclub the way he'd come.

Matt stopped short when he caught a glimpse of another man coming toward the building from the opposite direction. Reacting quickly, he ducked into a doorway, bringing Duchess with him.

He waited for what seemed like eons, but was barely a full minute, for the man to go past him on the opposite side of the street. Staying deep in the shadows, Matt was able to get a good look at the man's face.

The familiar features made him freeze.

No, it couldn't be. Matt held his breath, watching as the man's determined stride took him directly toward the nightclub.

When the guy was out of his field of vision, Matt edged closer, peeking around the corner just in time to see him walk up to the door leading downstairs to the lower level. He knocked twice, the door opened and he disappeared inside.

Matt stood there, trying to wrap his mind

around it. The man who'd just walked into the nightclub was none other than Judge Byron Dugan. The judge who'd presided, albeit for only one day, over his twin sister, Maddy's case against Alexander Pietro.

The judge whose name had been all over the news because he'd been receiving death threats.

Related to the blackmail scheme? Oh, yeah.

There was no denying it. Judge Dugan was involved in the gambling ring.

The fact that the judge was heading inside made him think there was a game starting any moment. Matt knew he needed to move fast if he wanted to catch them in the act.

FOURTEEN

Lacy felt vulnerable as she drove away, watching Matt and Duchess in the rearview mirror. There was no reason to be concerned. She knew Matt was armed and that he and Duchess were only attempting to track the gunman's scent, nothing more.

Still, it wasn't easy to shake off the niggling worry.

She turned the radio up and began to sing along with the happy rhythmic song. Thankfully, Rory was content enough to ride in the car, waving his arms and kicking his legs in the seat as if following along with the beat.

After several turns, she feared she might get lost, so she stopped singing and paid closer attention to the street signs. She didn't know this area very well. Her life had revolved around teaching, getting together for monthly book clubs with her teacher friends and checking in on her sister.

All of which seemed like a lifetime ago. Today,

in this moment, it was difficult to remember what her life had been like before Jill's murder.

Before Rory. And Matt.

Pushing thoughts of her tangled feelings for Matt aside, she focused on her surroundings. After another right turn, she found a familiar street and let out a relieved sigh. Even though she was a good five minutes early, she decided to head over to their designated meeting spot. Better to be early than lost and late.

The bright sunlight warmed the interior of the vehicle, so she shut off the engine and turned in her seat to check on Rory. The baby was gnawing on his fist, and she wondered if he was starting to cut teeth.

There was so much she didn't know about babies. When to start solid foods, when they began to teethe. She had a lot to learn, but didn't every new mother? It wasn't as if women were born with this type of knowledge imprinted in their brains.

Sitting and waiting for Matt and Duchess, time crawled by with incredible slowness. Five minutes passed and Matt still hadn't returned.

Tearing her gaze from the clock, she peered out at her surroundings, hoping to catch a glimpse of him and Duchess. But there was no sign of them. In fact, there was hardly any pedestrian traffic at all.

Another minute went by. She shifted in her seat, debating her options. Matt had instructed her to call his brothers for help, but surely nothing terrible had happened in broad daylight? She imagined she would be able to hear a gunshot from this close range.

She released her death-like grip on the steering wheel, straightening her fingers and forcing herself to take several deep breaths. Maybe Duchess had caught the gunman's scent and they'd followed it farther than Matt had anticipated.

Seven minutes past their meeting time, she finally saw Matt and Duchess approaching the vehicle. Her breath whooshed out in relief, and she forced a smile.

But her grin quickly faded as she caught the grim expression on Matt's face. She pushed the button to open the back hatch for Duchess, then scooted over the console so Matt could climb in behind the wheel.

"What happened?" she asked the minute he was seated.

"We need to get back to the motel, ASAP," he said. He didn't waste any time in pulling away from the curb and heading back toward the interstate. "I think there's a game in progress, and I want to catch them in the act."

Her mind spun at what he was saying. "Why do you think there's a game going on now?" Then it dawned on her, and she answered her own question. "You saw someone go inside."

"Not just someone," Matt corrected, glancing over at her. "Judge Byron Dugan."

"A judge?" She frowned. "Dugan? Isn't that the same guy who was getting death threats?"

"Yes. I was in the courtroom for the first day of the Pietro trial and remembered seeing him." Matt shook his head. "I still can't believe it. Judge Dugan is one of the best judges on the bench. He's fair and doesn't tolerate any nonsense. It's inconceivable to me that he's involved in this."

She hated seeing him so upset and reached out to rest her hand on his forearm. "No one is perfect, Matt. A good man can easily get swept up in an addiction."

"Yeah." He let out a harsh laugh. "I know you're right, but it's the illegal part that's sticking in my throat. A judge is sworn to uphold the law. What if he's used his judicial power to skew a case?"

"I'm not sure what to say." Lacy tightened her grip on his arm, wishing there was more she could do to make him feel better. "We have to believe that he maintained his integrity on the bench. It's possible this part of his life hasn't touched his professional side."

Matt clenched his jaw so tightly, she could see a small muscle pulsing at the corner of his mouth.

"Yeah, maybe. But something like this is bound to hang over his head like a dark cloud, tainting every decision he's made. The only consolation is that the DA's office made the deal with Pietro, not Dugan."

She couldn't argue—after all, the same thing would happen to a teacher. The barest hint of a scandal had far-reaching consequences.

They made it back to the motel in record time. She carried Rory's car seat inside, leaving Matt to take care of Duchess.

"So now what?" she asked, as she unbuckled Rory from the infant carrier.

Matt already had his phone to his ear. "Mike? I need backup. How soon can you get here?" There was a slight pause, then he added, "Okay, thirty minutes is reasonable. I'm going to need Mitch and Miles, too. Oh, and make sure you're armed. I'll explain everything once you get here."

Lacy picked up Rory, to comfort herself more than the baby. "What's the plan?"

"Arrest everyone involved in the gambling ring." Matt's voice was flat and clipped. She could tell he was still angry about the ramifications of arresting a judge.

And really, who's to say there weren't other high-profile people involved? Her stomach knotted with tension, and she remembered the initials in David's notebook.

Shifting Rory in her arms, she picked up the notebook. It was easy enough to find the initials J.B.D. She showed the notation to Matt. "This looks like it matches up with Judge Byron Dugan."

He scowled and punched in another phone number. "Do me a favor and see if you can find the initials for Assistant District Attorney Blake Ratcliff."

"Who is he?" she asked in confusion.

"A guy who tried to hurt my sister. It wouldn't surprise me to find out he's involved in this, too."

She sat on the edge of the bed and looked through the pages. Finding A.B.R. wasn't difficult, but there was no way to know for sure if they corresponded to Ratcliff.

"Mitch, it's Matt. Call me. I need backup." Matt punched more numbers into his phone, and this time, it sounded as if his brother answered. "Miles? I have new information and reason to believe that there's a game going on in the lower level of Secrets right now. Mike is meeting me here in thirty, can you make it, too?… Great, see you soon."

Matt set his phone aside and she frowned. "Shouldn't you call all of your brothers? There's no telling how many people are involved, but we do know several are cops."

He scrubbed his hands over his face, looking suddenly exhausted. "Yeah, you might be right. But Mitch is obviously tied up, and Marc is also up to his eyeballs in a hot case." He looked thoughtful for a moment, then reached for his phone. "I'll give Noah a call."

"Noah?" That name didn't sound familiar, and her stomach knotted at the thought of bringing in somebody who wasn't part of the family.

"My new brother-in-law. He's a cop, too."

"Oh, yes you mentioned you were partners before you went into K-9 training." Her relief didn't last long, though, as it sounded from Matt's side of the conversation like he wasn't close enough to help.

"It's okay, Noah, just meet us at the nightclub when you can, or maybe head out to the American Lodge instead. Thanks." Matt sighed. "So far I can only count on Mike and Miles for backup. Noah might get there, but he's almost an hour away. I was hoping to get one more. I don't like the thought of leaving you here alone."

Alone? She swallowed against a hard lump of fear that threatened to choke her. "I'm sure Rory and I will be all right."

Matt leaned over to pet Duchess. "I can leave Duchess here with you. She's a good protector."

"Are you sure?" She loved Duchess, but it seemed as if Matt might need her more than she would. "I would rather you have more backup.

Two guys, only one of them a cop, isn't going to be enough."

"We'll be okay," Matt assured her. "Mike actually went through the police academy, but decided at the last minute to drop out to start his own private investigator business. I've always thought there was some external reason that factored into his quitting, but he claims it was his choice. He told our father that he didn't like the idea of taking orders from others." Matt shrugged. "Regardless, he's trained as a cop, so there's truly nothing to worry about."

"Okay." Rory chose that moment to start fussing, and she realized it was well past time for his bottle.

She had just finished feeding Rory when Matt's brothers joined them. Both Mike and Miles looked serious as he filled them in on what had transpired in the short time he and Duchess had been outside the nightclub. He showed them the blueprints, indicating the entryway that led to the lower level.

"I can't believe they're meeting during the daytime," Miles said, rubbing the back of his neck. "It's Friday—shouldn't the judge be in court?"

"I have no idea how flexible their schedules are," Matt said. "But I know it was him."

"I'm going to need the notebook, Matt," Miles said. "I know you don't want to give it up, but…"

"It's fine." Matt handed the book to Miles. "Take it in as evidence."

"Will do," Miles agreed.

Lacy turned and went back through the connecting door to place Rory in the crib. He fussed for a moment, but once he settled down, she went back to join the Callahan brothers.

Mike glanced at her as she walked in through the connecting door. "Shouldn't someone stay here with Lacy and the baby?"

"I thought I'd leave Duchess behind. We weren't followed, so I think they'll be safe enough," Matt said. "And I asked Noah to head out this way when he has a chance. Give me a minute to strap on the dog's bulletproof vest."

At the sound of her name, Duchess wagged her tail and stood patiently while Matt buckled a vest over her chest and abdomen. When he finished, Lacy reached out to scratch the animal behind the ears. She attempted a smile. "I've seen Duchess in action. I'm sure we'll be fine."

Matt nodded. "I wouldn't leave you here if I didn't trust my partner. Guard, Duchess," he commanded. "Guard Lacy and Rory."

Duchess instantly sat at Lacy's side, her ears perked forward on alert.

"Ready to go?" Miles asked, his hand already on the doorknob. "We don't know how long the game will last."

"I'm ready," Matt said, but he was looking at her intently, as if he didn't want to leave.

Acting purely on instinct, she crossed over to wrap her arms around his neck. "Please be careful, Matt," she whispered.

He clutched her close. "I will."

She leaned back to look at him. "I'll pray for God to watch over you."

His green eyes bored into hers for a hard moment, then he swept her close and kissed her. She kissed him back, wishing he didn't have to go.

Miles coughed as if hiding a laugh, and Mike sighed. "We'll meet you outside," Mike said in a loud voice. "Just remember, you were the one in a hurry."

She was vaguely aware of the motel room door slamming shut behind them. Matt's kiss was wonderful, and when he finally raised his head, breathing hard, she rested her forehead on his chest.

"I'll be back as soon as possible," he promised in a low husky voice. "Call me if you need something."

I need you, she thought, but managed to stop herself from blurting out her feelings. This wasn't the time. Matt needed to concentrate on the danger he was about to face.

"I will." She forced herself to release her grip on his shoulders long enough to take a step back.

"Be safe, Matt. Call me when you have everything under control."

He nodded, looking as if he was about to say something more, but then silently turned away. He left the motel room to join his brothers outside.

Duchess paced the length of the room for a moment before coming back to sit beside Lacy. She rested her hand on the dog's glossy coat.

"He'll be back for us soon," she assured the dog. "You'll see."

Then she added a silent prayer. *Please, Lord, keep the Callahans safe from harm.*

Matt hated leaving Lacy and Rory behind, but taking them along to an illegal gambling bust wasn't an option.

"Give up the moony face already, would you?" Mike groused. "You're acting as if you'll never see her again."

Matt lightly punched his brother in the shoulder. "I don't have a moony face. Is it wrong to wish there was someone standing by to watch over her?"

"Hey, I know it's not easy," Miles said from the back seat. "But Duchess can hold her own."

Mike shook his head. "Man, you have it bad. Does Lacy have any idea how you feel about her?"

His chest tightened, but he strove to keep his

tone light. "I care about her as a friend, okay? Enough about my personal life, let's focus on breaking up this gambling ring. We still need to figure out who's responsible for murdering Williams and attempting to shoot Lacy."

"By the way, I participated in the Williams autopsy early this morning," Miles said. "The ME is convinced Williams died the night before Lacy took off with Rory."

"Wait, what?" Matt locked gazes with his brothers in the mirror. "Is he sure?"

"*She's* positive," Miles corrected. "There's a new female pathologist working in the ME's office, Dr. Grace Goldberg, and she seems to know what she's doing. She puts the time of death almost twenty-four hours before Jill's murder."

Matt turned his attention toward the road, his mind whirling with possibilities. "I don't understand," he said. "Lacy heard the argument that preceded the murder. She repeated it to me twice."

There was a long silence before Miles spoke up. "Don't you think it's possible that Jill was murdered by the same gunman who tried to finish Lacy off at the convenience store? The same guy who followed her trail to the cabin? Maybe he thinks she can identify him?"

He felt as if someone had body slammed him against the wall. Of course, his brother's theory made sense. Why hadn't he thought of that possibility before?

"The guy said something to Jill about telling him the truth." Matt glanced at Miles again. "At the time, Lacy had thought it was related to David's assumption that she was being unfaithful, but if Williams was already dead, then the gunman was likely looking for the notebook. The truth about the blackmail scheme."

"Exactly," Miles agreed.

The pieces of the puzzle fit, except for... "What about the Amber Alert?" he asked. "Lacy assumed that David was the one to put out the alert in an attempt to get custody and to pin the murder on her, but why would one of his cop buddies do that?"

"Same reason," Mike pointed out. "The dude wanted a good reason to arrest her. If the same guy killed David, he could easily claim that Williams was afraid Lacy would try to get Rory away from Jill. That Lacy influenced her sister and convinced her to file for divorce. I imagine he would want to cover his tracks by pretending David was still alive and well."

"Makes sense," Matt agreed. "I wish I knew which cop was the shooter."

"You have it narrowed down to three possibilities, don't you?" Miles asked.

"Hugh Nichols, Jeff Jones and Randal Whalen." Matt exited the interstate and headed for the same place he'd used as a meeting spot with Lacy ninety minutes ago. "We found all three of their initials in the notebook."

"Okay, then," Miles said, crossing his arms over his chest. "We'll focus on the three of them. Would make our job easier if they all happened to be at the club today."

"Yeah." But Matt wasn't holding out much hope that it would be that easy. His motto was to hope for the best while preparing for the worst. He threw the SUV into Park and shut down the engine. "We'll walk in from here."

"How do you want to do this?" Mike asked once they were all standing outside beside the vehicle.

"Two of us go in from the back doorway, the one Judge Dugan used to access the building. The third guy goes in from the front, in case they scatter."

"I'll go in with you," Miles offered, slapping Matt on the back. "Since we're both working the case, it only makes sense for us to stick together. Mike, take the front."

Mike shrugged. "Fine with me."

Matt hesitated, unable to shake the sense that he was missing something. He shrugged off the sensation, assuming that the reason he was feeling off was because Duchess wasn't there. He'd grown used to working with his K-9 partner, and it felt odd to be without her.

"This way." He took off down the street to the corner. "The back door is straight ahead," he said to Miles. "Mike, you'll want to go down another block to the front of the building. We'll breach the doors in exactly ten minutes. Ready?"

"Ready," Miles and Mike agreed simultaneously.

Mike set off at a jog while he and Miles approached the back entranceway. There weren't many people around, thankfully, since the nightclub didn't open for a few hours yet.

He took the lead position on the right side of the door, leaving Miles on the left. They flattened themselves against the building and waited.

Exactly ten minutes later, Miles gave him a nod. Matt kicked in the door and went in first, holding his weapon ready. There was an identical sound of a door bursting open from the front simultaneously.

He could hear voices questioning what was going on in response to his and Mike's noisy entrance into the building. Matt clamored down the stairs. "Police!" he shouted. "We have the place surrounded. You're all under arrest. Hands in the air! Now!"

There were three gaming tables, but only one was in use. Five men, including the judge, were rising from their seats around it, a large pile of cash heaped in the center, mostly one hundred dollar bills. Cards flew as the men attempted to flee, one heading for the staircase along the wall that would take him right toward Mike.

A shot rang out, and Matt dropped to one knee. He took aim at the shooter, recognizing him as police officer Jeff Jones. "Drop it!" he shouted, then when the guy didn't listen, pulled the trigger. Jones fell to the floor with a cry.

One down, four to go. But he didn't see the other two cops, Hugh Nichols or Randal Whalen.

Chaos erupted, but it didn't take long for the three Callahans to apprehend the poker players. But even after they had read them their rights and cuffed them, he knew this mess wasn't over.

In fact, it might only be the beginning.

Two officers were still at large. He needed to apprehend them before deeming Lacy and Rory safe.

FIFTEEN

As Lacy walked the length of the motel room holding Rory, back and forth, over and over, Duchess kept pace, close at her side. So close that she almost tripped over the animal. Twice.

She found herself talking to the dog like she spoke to Rory. "Sorry, girl, but give me a little room, okay?"

Duchess didn't seem to get it, nudging her thigh with her nose as if to tell her to keep walking.

So she did. Rory was being unusually fussy. She jiggled him in her arms as she paced in an attempt to calm him down. When that didn't work, she tried giving him a bottle. Unfortunately, that didn't help, either.

Being left alone to care for Rory caused her insecurities to return. She had thought she'd been doing a fairly decent job of taking care of him, but of course five minutes after Matt and his brothers had left, Rory had begun to cry.

"Shh, it's okay, I'm here. You're fine, everything's going to be all right."

He only cried louder, pitiful wails that she had no idea how to fix. What was wrong with him? Why was he crying? Was he missing Matt? Or worse, had he finally realized that she was all he had left in the world?

She battled back a wave of helplessness. She'd been overwhelmed before, and there was no reason to fall back on the old feelings of inadequacy.

She could handle this. Lots of women did this every day. She might make mistakes, but she and Rory would figure things out, together.

Feeling more self-confident, she continued pacing for another ten minutes before setting him down to change his diaper. Once that was finished, she walked the room some more, then decided to lay him down in the center of the bed on his stomach. Babies sometimes had gas pains, so maybe lying down would help.

Rory stretched and rolled from side to side, then finally, thankfully, stopped crying.

She'd done just fine. She didn't need Matt or anyone else to help her out. She could do it on her own.

On the heels of that thought came another. She might not need Matt's help with Rory, but the thought of not seeing him again once this was over left her feeling sad and alone. The sadness she could understand; after all, they'd been through a lot together. But the loneliness? That was just crazy. She hadn't been seeing anyone before meeting Matt and, frankly, hadn't wanted to. Normally she didn't trust men, didn't believe that the kindness they showed to the world didn't also hide a dark temper. Yet nothing about the time that she'd spent with Matt was normal.

How could she miss a man she barely knew? A man she'd come to care about far more than she should have?

Duchess sat straight and tall at the foot of the bed, as if instinctively knowing the infant was an important part of her protection detail. She looked like a furry sentinel, especially with the way her ears perked forward. Lacy smiled and rubbed the silky spot at the nape of Duchess's neck.

"Good girl," she whispered. "I'm glad you're here."

Duchess licked her arm, but didn't move from her spot. Lacy watched as Rory wiggled around a bit, then rolled over onto his back. The crying must have tuckered him out, because he finally closed his wide blue eyes and drifted off to sleep.

Lacy's shoulders slumped in relief. Giving herself a pep talk was one thing, but fully believing in herself was another. She couldn't help wondering how many more instances like this she would face over the next, say, eighteen years.

Don't go there. One day at a time.

As a teacher, she knew how to deal with fifth graders, so really, all she needed was a few more years with Rory and the rest would come naturally. Isn't that how all parents coped?

Of course, it was.

Wearily, she rose to her feet, glancing around the cluttered motel room. Probably best to clean this mess up now, but then again, wasn't the advice given to new mothers to rest while the baby slept?

Maybe she should give it a try.

She glanced down at Rory again, realizing she couldn't leave him in the bed. If he woke up and began to roll again, he might fall off.

Gingerly, very gingerly, she eased her hands beneath his sleeping body, hoping and praying he wouldn't wake up. Lifting him up, she carried him the few steps over to the crib, letting her breath out in a silent whoosh when he continued sleeping.

One task accomplished. Ignoring the mess, she stretched out on the bed and closed her eyes. She wasn't good at taking naps, but obviously this was one skill she would need to work on.

It seemed like only a few seconds that she'd had her eyes closed when Duchess began to growl. She blinked and sat up, feeling groggy. The light shining between the drapes over the window was different, so some time had passed, although she didn't think it was much more than thirty or forty minutes.

A spike of fear stabbed deep when she saw Duchess standing at the door of the motel room, low, continuous growls coming from her throat.

Any other dog and she might assume the person outside was a maid, or maybe some guy delivering pizza to the room next door, but not Duchess. She never growled.

Except when there was potential danger.

Lacy's thoughts turned razor sharp and she leaped into action, grabbing the shawl and picking up Rory from the crib. She wrapped him tightly against her body, the same way she'd done the night of Jill's murder. The parallel between that night and today felt frighteningly real.

Only this time, she couldn't risk running outside. The only way out would take her directly past the gunman.

Which meant she and Rory were trapped inside, with little to no place to hide.

She swept the mobile phone off the bedside table and held her breath as she squeezed past Duchess and ducked through the connecting door into Matt's motel room. Feeling guilty at leaving Duchess behind, she closed the connecting door and slid the dead bolt in place. Then she sought refuge in the bathroom, closing and locking that door behind her, too.

She stepped into the tub and sank down until she was reclined against the cold ceramic, keeping low. Despite the two closed doors, she could hear Duchess's growls getting louder and more insistent.

Frantic, she dialed Matt's number and listened to the endless ringing on the other end of the line. When he didn't pick up she disconnected and tried Miles. Then Mike—both with the same results. Finally, she called 911.

The muffled sounds of loud banging on the motel room door reached her ears, and she winced when they were followed by Duchess's sharp staccato barks.

"911, what's your emergency?"

"Someone is breaking into my motel room." She kept her voice low, even though she knew it wouldn't take long for the intruder to find her in the bathroom. Sure, she'd given herself an extra couple of minutes, but once he'd cleared her room, he'd make short work of the connecting door.

But where else could she go?

The dispatcher repeated her request. "I'm at the American Lodge motel, room three. Please hurry!"

"Is the intruder armed?" the operator asked.

Lacy could hear clicking keys in the background and hoped that meant the woman wasn't just chatting, but had already sent a message to alert the closest police officer to the danger.

There was another loud bang against the door, and she imagined the gunman kicking it in. How long would it hold?

Not long enough.

"I don't know! Hurry! I'm alone with a baby and a K-9 officer. I'm afraid he's going to kill us!" She wanted to scream, but forced her voice to remain soft and quiet.

"Please stay on the line," the dispatcher said in her cool, controlled tone.

Another loud bang and the sound of splintering wood. A yelp of pain made her think Duchess may have gotten a piece of the guy. She sucked in a harsh breath, her heart jackhammering in her chest.

She held Rory protectively, turning so that her back was facing the door, shielding him as much as she was able to with her own body.

"Hurry," she begged the dispatcher. "I think he's inside the motel now. Please hurry."

For some odd reason, Rory didn't cry, maybe because he was all cried out from his earlier fussiness. Or maybe he instinctively knew that they needed to be quiet. She pressed her mouth against the downy softness of his hair, closed her eyes and began to pray, repeating the words frantically over and over in her mind.

Lord, spare this child's life. Please keep him safe in Your care!

At Secrets, the five men, including the one who'd tried to escape out the front door, were easily subdued. Judge Dugan hung his head in shame, especially once he'd recognized Matt as Maddy's twin.

Matt kept his distance from the judge, hoping this arrest wouldn't cast doubts on all the cases Judge Dugan had presided over. He pulled out his phone, intending to alert his sister so she would be prepared before any of this hit the news, when he saw the missed call from the disposable phone he'd given Lacy.

He quickly pressed his thumb on the number in an attempt to return the call, but she didn't pick up.

Not good.

"I missed Lacy's call," Matt told Miles. "We need to get back to the motel right away."

"You go with Mike. I'll stay here to wrap this up," Miles said.

Matt wasn't about to waste another second. "Mike! Now!" He took off running up the stairs to the street level, barely hearing Mike's footsteps behind him. Outside, he sprinted toward the SUV. When he reached the driver's seat, he wrenched open the door and jumped in behind the wheel. His brother managed to stagger into the passenger side before he hit the gas and shot out onto the road.

"Thanks for waiting," Mike said in a dry tone. "I wouldn't want to hold you up or anything."

"The other two cops are unaccounted for and I missed a call from Lacy," Matt said. "What if they figured out where she was? What if their plan was to set up this game to distract us? Then head out to the motel with the intent of silencing her once and for all?"

"Duchess will protect her," Mike said in a soft, reassuring tone. The hint of joking had vanished. "And we'll be there soon."

"I know. I'm trying to have faith in God's plan." Matt hated the thought of Duchess facing potentially two gunmen on her own. He'd thought for sure that at least two of the cops would have been at the poker game. Three hadn't been likely, but two had seemed plausible. One thing he hadn't seriously considered was the idea that two of the cops had bonded enough to work together.

He mentally berated himself for not doing as he'd promised himself, preparing for the worst.

He pressed down hard on the accelerator, the sense of worry blooming larger in his chest. He'd felt as if something was off earlier, and maybe this was it. A poker game during the day, especially during the week, had been nothing more than a clever ruse. A trap to get Lacy and Rory alone.

Hang on, Lacy. I'm coming!

The houses passed by in a blur. The exit came up quickly, and he slowed enough to get safely off the interstate. The motel wasn't far now, and he tightened his grip on the steering wheel, praying he wasn't too late.

The long, white two-story motel loomed ahead, and he watched in horror as a man with dirty blond hair lifted his leg and kicked at Lacy's motel room door. In the nanosecond during which he'd gotten a glimpse of the man's profile, Matt knew he wasn't the same perp who'd gone after Lacy with a gun. He was wearing off-duty black jeans and a black leather jacket.

"No!" Matt shouted, when the motel room door shuddered beneath the force of the guy's heel. Where was the motel manager? Why wasn't anyone else out there helping?

His brother rolled down the window and aimed his Glock toward the intruder. Mike fired a round, but they were moving too fast for accuracy.

The intruder ducked and kicked again. This time the frame broke and the door snapped open. He could hear Duchess barking, then heard a shout of pain from the intruder.

Bitter fear for Duchess coated his tongue, and he steered erratically into the parking lot and abruptly stopped the car.

Mike was out in a flash, with Matt hard on his heels. They heard a gunshot, and his heart squeezed painfully.

"Duchess!" Matt screamed. He knew his partner would protect Lacy and Rory with her life if necessary. The night that the gunman had sliced her with a knife burned in his mind.

Mike reached the door first and the gunman staggered around to face him. Duchess had her jaw latched around his ankle, hard enough to draw blood. He couldn't see any blood marring the animal's coat, but that didn't mean she hadn't taken a bullet. Had the vest protected her?

Before Matt could say anything, Mike lashed out with his foot in some sort of weird martial arts move that Matt had never seen before, kicking the gun right out of the guy's hand. Then Mike lifted his Glock, pointing it squarely at the cop's chest. "Don't move."

"Hands up!" Matt said, finding his voice. "Which one are you, Randal Whalen or Hugh Nichols?"

The guy's eyes widened in shocked surprise. "Whalen," he grudgingly admitted.

If this was Randal Whalen, that left Hugh Nichols as the original gunman—the one who'd tried to kill Lacy outside the convenience store. Had these two idiots decided to work together after all? If so, where was Nichols?

Matt stepped close enough to grab the man's wallet out of his back pocket to verify he was Whalen. "Duchess, Release."

Duchess let go and backed away, growling fiercely. "Guard, Duchess," he commanded, before turning his attention to the cop. "Randal Whalen, you're under arrest for attempted murder of a police officer and participating in an underground gambling ring. Oh, and I reserve the right to bring other charges forward at a future date."

The man who'd kicked in the door lifted his arms up over his head. "I'm gonna sue. That dog bit me. You gotta take me to the hospital, man, I can hardly walk. I might get rabies."

"Duchess is the one who should be taken in to be examined," Mike shot back. "We don't know what kind of diseases you've got running through your bloodstream."

Mike's remark made Matt smile grimly. "Duchess, Come."

His partner loped toward him, and Matt nearly wept with relief when she appeared unharmed. He sent up a silent prayer of thanks to God for keeping his partner, Lacy and Rory all safe.

"Cuff him and take him outside," Matt said,

tossing his handcuffs to his brother. "I need to check on Lacy and Rory."

"My pleasure." Mike caught the cuffs one-handed. Apparently, his reflexes had been honed by whatever martial arts he was practicing these days. Matt waited until he knew that the cop was securely restrained.

"Duchess, Come." He crossed the threshold into the motel room, sweeping his gaze over the area. There was a lot of stuff around, but no sign of either Lacy or Rory. A sliver of unease worked its way under his skin.

"Lacy? It's Matt. Are you okay?"

The room was empty; the bathroom door was open and the interior was dark. He glanced over, noticing how the connecting door between their rooms was closed from the opposite side. When he pushed against it, he found it was locked. Good thinking on her part, he thought with a grim smile.

"Lacy? It's safe! You can come out now!" he called loudly. Pressing his ear to the door, he listened, but didn't hear anything. If she was hiding in the bathroom, which is exactly where he would have gone if he were in her shoes, then she might not have been able to hear him. Duchess stood patiently while he dug in his pocket for his own room key. No reason he couldn't go in through the main door.

He moved past the broken door to head outside. He stopped abruptly when he saw a police squad parked beside his SUV, blocking the view from the lobby area of the motel. The red and blue lights weren't flashing the way they should have been during an emergency response.

Then he swallowed hard when he noticed the tall man with familiar features standing in full uniform, holding a gun pointed directly at Mike. He took a step back, but it was a fraction of a second too late.

"Don't move, Callahan," the guy called. "Put your hands up where I can see them."

He did as instructed, realizing this was the same man who'd leveled a gun at Lacy outside the convenience store. Who'd sliced Duchess with his knife and had shot at Matt outside the cabin. And the way things stood right now, anyone looking over here would assume that he and Mike were the criminals, not the other way around.

Had the 911 operator called him to the scene? Or had this been part of his and Whalen's plan?

Either way, it was clear Officer Hugh Nichols had found them.

SIXTEEN

When Lacy heard the reassuring sound of Matt's voice, she let out a long sigh of relief.

It was over. Matt was here, and she was sure he'd brought along at least one of his brothers. Whatever had transpired at the nightclub hadn't taken long.

She rolled on her back in the bathtub, holding Rory against her, then awkwardly rose up to a partial sitting position. With Rory bound against her, she couldn't bend at the waist, so she threw one leg over the edge of the tub and then grabbed on to the sink in an attempt to haul herself upright.

It wasn't pretty, but she managed to leverage herself out of the ceramic tub. *This must be similar to how it would feel to be pregnant*, she thought with a wry smile. She hadn't really entertained the idea of having a child of her own, since she'd never trusted a man long enough to get to the point of considering even a long-term relationship. But spending the past few days with Matt had given her all kinds of ideas related to the future.

Ideas of seeing him again, once the danger was over.

If he was even interested, which she wasn't sure he was. Oh, he'd kissed her, not once but three times! But that might not mean much. After losing his girlfriend and her child, he wasn't likely to be in the market for a relationship. He was probably just being nice to her.

Enough. This wasn't the time or place to think about what might happen tomorrow. In fact, she had other, more pressing, priorities. Such as working with Social Services to begin the adoption process so she could keep Rory. Somehow, she didn't think her sister had gotten around to making a will. If Jill had, she'd never mentioned it.

Shaking off the distressing thoughts, she opened the bathroom door and poked her head out to survey the room. She expected to see Matt there, but the room was empty. The connecting door was still closed and appeared to be locked, the way she'd left it.

A trickle of unease raised the hair on the back of her neck. Where was Matt? She'd heard his voice.

Surely, he hadn't left her and Rory behind?

She took several tentative steps forward. The silence was eerie and strangely threatening. Approaching the window, she could hear the low rumble of deep voices, and through a gap in the curtains she saw a police car outside.

For some odd reason, the lights on the rack along the top of the car weren't flashing, which wasn't reassuring. She slipped closer to the opening between the curtains to get a better look at what was going on.

She froze when she realized Matt was standing there with his hands up in the air. A cop dressed in full uniform, no doubt the one who'd arrived in the patrol car, was standing several feet away, pointing a gun toward Matt. Mike was there, too, also holding his hands up in a gesture of surrender.

What was going on? And where were the motel staff? Although, it occurred to her that the cop dressed in uniform would hardly be viewed as the bad guy.

In fact, quite the opposite.

Easing back from the curtains, Lacy swallowed hard and tried to figure out what she should do. She could call 911 again, but what if the next cop to arrive was an enemy as well? There could easily be others.

She hadn't seen Duchess, either, which was weird. Surely, Duchess would stay near Matt?

Unless— Her gaze landed on the connecting door. She silently unlocked the dead bolt and inched the door open.

Duchess hovered near the broken door of the motel room, hugging the wall and apparently out of sight from the men standing outside. Duchess must have caught Lacy's scent through the crack in the doorway, because the animal turned and came over to sniff at the opening.

Lacy eased the door open enough for her to get her fingers through. She lightly stroked Duchess's fur, grateful to see that she appeared unharmed. But the dog didn't stay near the connecting doorway. She turned and softly padded over to stand near the broken door, as if awaiting a signal.

Was Matt able to see Duchess? If so, he might be able to use her help. Having Duchess, a trained K-9 officer, available meant they weren't completely sunk, not yet. But it wouldn't take long. She scooted closer to the window, hoping to overhear what they were saying.

"I'm telling you, he has a dog! It attacked me," a whiney male voice said.

"You hurt my partner," Matt said in a sharp tone. "Don't you think she would be out here if she wasn't hurt?"

Lacy could tell Matt was trying to buy them time, but for what?

"Where is it? I want that notebook now!" The

deep male voice of the cop holding the gun sent goosebumps along her arms. It was him! His voice was the one she'd overheard the night of Jill's murder.

All this time, she'd assumed the intruder was David, but she'd been wrong. David hadn't killed Jill.

It was the man standing outside, wearing a full cop uniform, who'd committed the murder.

All because of David's notebook.

She felt sick to her stomach, knowing that Jill had died for nothing more than greed.

So now what? She needed desperately to find some sort of diversion. As much as she didn't want to close the connecting door, she knew it was probably for the best. The last thing she wanted was to get between Duchess and Matt.

She was glad Matt had given the notebook to Miles, although handing it over wasn't likely to get them out of this.

The cop had been searching for her, no doubt because he knew she would be able to recognize his voice as the man who'd murdered Jill. Matt would stall as long as he could, attempting to convince the cop that she and Rory weren't here.

But eventually the situation would unravel, and she and Rory might be exposed.

She glanced toward the bathroom, wondering

if she should hide in there with Rory. The baby deserved to be safe from harm, didn't he?

A movement from outside caught her attention. She eased closer to the window, being careful not to be seen.

There it was again. A figure was crouched behind the squad car. The brown hair looked familiar.

Miles! Matt's brother had come to rescue them.

But how could she get the news to Matt? A text message? No, he couldn't look at his phone.

She needed a diversion. What could she toss outside to cause a distraction?

There were two small, fist-sized glasses in the bathroom. She picked one up, leaving the other behind. Returning to the center of the room, she assessed her options.

Tossing it out through the open doorway of the adjacent room was her best bet. That way, she could use this room as a refuge, at least for a few minutes.

Should she leave Rory in the bathtub? The idea of being separated from him didn't sit well, but better that than risk having him hit by a stray bullet. She set the glass down and began to unwrap the shawl. When she finished, she tucked it around Rory in the tub as a cushion. He cried a little but then thankfully settled down.

Lacy unlocked the connecting door and opened

it. Then she picked up the glass and slipped through into the motel room where Duchess still waited patiently for Matt's signal. Being this close to the broken doorway was scary, but she pushed past her fear long enough to find a spot where she could see through the narrow opening.

Once she identified her target, an open spot of the parking lot, she brought her arm back and threw the glass with all her might. Before she heard the glass shatter against the concrete pavement, she was already making her way back through the connecting doorway.

The rest was up to Matt, Duchess, Miles—and God.

"I don't have the notebook," Matt insisted for what felt like the tenth time in less than five minutes. Although, truthfully, every minute was a gift. He hoped and prayed either Miles or Noah would show up soon. "I've given the notebook over to the authorities, so there's no point in holding us at gunpoint, Nichols. The gig is up. Game over. We've already arrested Judge Dugan and the others involved in the poker game less than an hour ago."

"I know you have the notebook, Callahan," Nichols sneered. "Stalling is a waste of time. Maybe I'll shoot your brother in the kneecap, a painful but not lethal wound. Just something to show I mean business."

The barrel of Nichols's gun shifted toward Mike. Matt knew he couldn't wait a moment longer. It was now or never.

He gave Duchess the hand signal for Attack at the exact same time he heard the distinct sound of glass shattering somewhere off to his left.

From there, several things transpired at once. Miles jumped out from behind the squad car at the same second Duchess sprinted toward Nichols. The first cop that they'd cuffed, Randal Whalen, took off running away from the scene. The sound of gunfire echoed around him. There was a burning sensation in his left leg, but he ignored the pain. He hit the pavement and rolled toward Mike, wishing desperately that he had a backup weapon.

"Matt!" Mike's shout caused him to lift his head. A small pistol came flying through the air toward him, and he caught it with his right hand. In a smooth motion, he turned and aimed at Nichols.

But he didn't shoot. Couldn't, not without risking his partner. Duchess and Nichols were rolling around on the ground, Duchess's jaw latched onto the cop's shoulder in a firm hold. Unfortunately, Nichols was still holding on to his gun, attempting to angle it around so that he could shoot the animal.

"No!" Matt shouted hoarsely. He staggered to his feet, wincing as pain shot through him. Blood ran down his leg, but he managed to get closer to where Duchess and Nichols fought for their lives.

"Stay back," Miles ordered.

Matt came to an abrupt stop but couldn't tear his gaze away from Duchess. If anything happened to his partner, he knew it would be his fault. It was bad enough that Nichols had hurt Duchess before.

Out of nowhere, Mike's foot lashed through his field of vision, kicking the gun right out from Nichols's hand and sending it spinning across the asphalt parking lot.

"Don't move," Miles said, placing the barrel of his gun against Nichols's right temple.

"Release! Heel," Matt ordered. Duchess responded instantly, releasing her grip on Nichols's shoulder and spinning away from the assailant, returning to Matt's side. "Good girl," he praised, leaning down to give her coat a nice rub.

"She okay?" Mike asked.

He nodded. "Yes, thanks to you. I want to know where you learned martial arts. Those moves are nice and handy."

"Where did Whalen go?" Mike demanded.

"Good question." Matt took one step, then another. "Unfortunately, I'm in no condition to track him down."

"I'll get him," Mike said. "He's handcuffed, so he won't get far."

"Hugh Nichols, you're under arrest for the murder of David Williams and Jill Williams," Miles said, as he tossed a pair of handcuffs to Mike. "You have the right to remain silent. Anything you say can and will be used against you in a court of law. You have the right to an attorney..."

Matt's vision blurred and he suddenly felt light-headed. He blinked, trying to focus.

"Looks like you guys have everything under control," Noah said, stepping out from behind the SUV. Matt stared at his brother-in-law for a moment, wondering where in the world he'd come from.

"Yeah, you're late as usual," Mike said in a dry tone. "How does Maddy put up with you?"

"She loves me," Noah said, putting his hand over his heart. Then his tone changed to one of concern. "Hey, Matt, are you okay? You're losing a fair amount of blood over there."

"I am?" He glanced down, realizing there was a dark reddish-brown puddle forming on the ground around his left foot. Noah was right—the pool of blood was getting larger and larger.

The earth tilted again and Matt felt himself

slipping downward. Strong arms supported him, easing him slowly onto the pavement.

"Call an ambulance!" Noah shouted.

Matt reached up to grab Noah's shirt. "Grab the key out of my pocket," he said in an urgent tone.

"Huh?" Noah looked confused. "Hey, just relax, okay, Matt? I'll take good care of you. Maddy would never forgive me if I let something happen to you."

Matt closed his eyes for a moment, fighting the dizziness. He needed to stay conscious. "Listen! Lacy and Rory are inside the motel room. Someone needs to go inside to make sure they're okay. Use my key."

"I'll do it." Miles slid the room key out of Matt's back pocket and held it up. "I'll take good care of Lacy and Rory. Just stay put for a minute. The ambulance is on its way."

Matt struggled to remain conscious, determined to see for himself that Lacy and Rory were unharmed. Against his will, his eyelids slipped closed.

"Matt!" Lacy's voice roused him, and he forced his eyes open with superhuman effort. He saw Lacy standing there, clutching Rory to her chest. "It worked. My diversion worked!"

Diversion? At first he didn't understand, but

then he remembered the sound of breaking glass. He hadn't realized Lacy had been the source.

"You were great." Matt squinted up at her. "Are you and Rory okay?" he asked, blinking in an effort to keep her in focus. "You're not hurt?"

"We're fine," she assured him. She knelt beside him, her lips soft against his forehead. "God was watching over all of us today."

"Yeah," he agreed in a faint tone. He'd saved Lacy and Rory, despite being unable to save Carly.

Was this part of God's plan? Debra breaking up with him so he would be there to help keep Rory and Lacy safe from the gunman? From Hugh Nichols?

"He's losing a lot of blood," Miles said, coming over to kneel beside him.

"I'm right here," Matt managed to say. "I can still hear you. Why are you guys talking about me as if I'm already dead?"

"Of course you're not dead. But you are seriously injured. The bullet must have nicked your artery," Lacy said in a worried tone. "We need to place a tourniquet above the wound in an attempt to slow down the blood loss."

Matt was vaguely aware of his belt being slipped out of the loops and wrapped around the top of his thigh. He groaned in pain, clenching his jaw as Noah cinched it tight.

Boy did that hurt. Worse than getting shot.

"Keep it in place for five minutes, then loosen for a minute," Lacy instructed. "Keep repeating the pattern until the ambulance arrives."

He didn't like feeling helpless. There was still work to be done. Had Mike caught up to Whalen? He certainly hoped so.

Duchess licked his cheek, making him smile, despite the way his leg felt as if it were being seared by a bonfire.

Focus, he reminded himself. "Someone hasta take care of Duchess…" His voice trailed off as weakness overpowered his determination.

"Shh, it's okay. I'll take care of Duchess," Lacy said, putting her hand on his cheek. "Rest now, the ambulance is almost here. It just got off the interstate."

"Lacy," he whispered. There was something important he needed to tell her. What was it? He couldn't corral his scattered thoughts.

"I'm here, Matt." Her voice was beautifully melodic, and it pained him to realize he might not get a chance to hear it again. "You're going to be fine, you hear me? The ambulance crew is here and they're going to take you to the best hospital in the city."

"Lacy, I lo…" His voice trailed off and he knew staying awake was a lost cause. He simply couldn't hold back the darkness for a moment longer.

Time to stop fighting against the inevitable. He relaxed and let go, giving himself up into God's care.

SEVENTEEN

"Matt? Can you hear me?" Lacy watched in horror as Matt's eyes closed and his face went slack. "Matt?"

"Hey, it's okay, he still has a pulse," Noah said in a tone that she assumed was meant to be reassuring. She didn't like the pallor in Matt's face, though. "We need to give the paramedics room to work."

Hugging Rory to her chest with one arm, she clung to Matt's hand with the other, reluctant to let him go. He'd lost so much blood… She shuddered at the possibility of losing him.

"Come on, Lacy." Noah gently placed his hand under her elbow, helping her upright. "The danger is over. We have both Hugh Nichols and Randal Whalen in custody."

"You do?" Dazed, she looked around the parking lot of the American Lodge, surprised to realize Mike had returned with Whalen in tow.

It really was over, although not without casualties. Matt's gunshot wound was the most serious, since Nichols's shoulder injuries proved to be superficial and Whalen's ankle hadn't been bad enough to stop him from running away.

More police officers had arrived on the scene, and she could see that Mike and Miles were in deep conversation with them, no doubt providing a detailed timeline of the events that had taken place over the past thirty minutes or so.

Thirty minutes that had seemed like a lifetime.

As she watched the paramedics work over Matt, providing badly needed fluids, Rory began to fuss, waving his arms and legs as if tired of being held. She shifted him in her arms, grateful for the fact that he'd waited until now to show his displeasure. He'd been amazingly quiet while they'd hid in the bathroom, keeping them safe.

"Do you need something?" Noah asked. "You want me to hold him for a bit?"

She hesitated, then nodded. Matt was right about learning to accept help when it was available. Her desperate need to remain independent seemed foolish now. "I'd appreciate it if you could take him long enough for me to make a bottle."

"No problem." Noah took the baby, then lifted Rory high in the air, distracting him from his hunger and making him giggle. She ducked through the broken doorway to find the formula and the bottles. When she returned outside, she caught a glimpse of Matt stretched out on a gurney, sliding into the back of the ambulance.

"Wait!" she called out, rushing toward the paramedics. "You're taking him to Trinity Medical Center, right?"

"Yes, ma'am," the paramedic said with a nod.

The tightness across her chest eased. She was glad they were taking him to the level-one trauma center. "Okay, thanks."

She stepped back, watching as they shut the ambulance doors and pulled away, red lights flashing and sirens screaming. She didn't move until they approached the highway.

When she felt Noah's presence beside her, she turned toward him. "Here, I'll take him."

"Sure." Noah handed Rory over, then jammed his hands into his pockets. "Listen, a Detective Styles just showed up, along with Matt's boss, Lieutenant Gray. Miles is soothing the lieutenant's ruffled feathers, but Styles needs your statement."

"Okay. I can talk while giving Rory his bottle, but I need to sit down." Exhaustion had hit hard, so she headed back inside the motel room to find a place to sit. Less than a minute later, Detective Styles came in and introduced himself.

After asking some basic questions, such as her name, age and occupation, he requested she start at the beginning—the night she'd overheard her sister's murder and had taken off running. It seemed as if that night had been months ago instead of days, but she reiterated the events that were seared into her memory.

The interview took much longer than she'd anticipated. In fact, he might have continued firing questions at her if not for Rory needing to have his diaper changed.

"Excuse me," she said, rising to her feet. "I have to take care of my nephew. Can we continue this at a later time? It's getting dark, and I need to get over to the hospital to check on Matt, er, Officer Callahan."

"Uh, yeah, okay." The detective seemed a bit annoyed but didn't argue. "Here's my card. I need to know how to reach you."

That comment brought her up short. Where was she going to stay now that the danger was over? Her single bedroom apartment?

And what about Duchess? She'd promised Matt she'd take care of her while he was in the hospital.

Her mind whirled as she changed Rory, considering her options. For now, her best bet was probably to go back to Jill's place if the police had finished processing it as a crime scene. That's where all Rory's things were, and she could sleep on the futon again.

"Lacy?" Mike poked his head through the doorway. "Are you ready to go? I thought you'd like to stop at the hospital for a bit before you head home."

"Yes, but give me five minutes to get everything together." Lacy placed Rory in his car seat and then packed what was left of the diapers, formula and bottles into a plastic bag.

Outside, she found Mike, Miles and Noah deep in conversation. Whatever they were discussing ended abruptly when she approached.

"Lacy, we think it's best if you stay at Matt's house for the next few days," Miles said. "Gives us time to take turns checking in on you, Rory and Duchess. I've turned over all the evidence to Styles, who's taking over the case. Matt's boss isn't happy with us—not that I care."

She was taken aback by their offer but quickly nodded in agreement. Truthfully, she liked their idea better, since she wasn't sure she had the option of staying at Jill's. "Thank you, I'd appreciate that."

"Good. Let's stop there on the way to the hospital."

The next few hours passed in a blur. She left Rory's things at Matt's house, fed Duchess and then caught a ride to the hospital with Mike. But Matt was still in surgery and Rory grew even more fussy, so in the end she accepted Mike's offer to return to Matt's place, providing Rory the opportunity for a good night's sleep.

She stayed in the guest bedroom, and Duchess remained close at hand, but she still felt as if she were intruding in Matt's personal space. Rory fell asleep quickly, but she was wide-awake, worrying about Matt. When the phone rang at ten o'clock at night, she quickly answered it.

"Lacy? It's Mike. Just wanted to let you know Matt is out of surgery and doing fine. The artery was repaired and he was given a few units of blood. He looks great."

She closed her eyes on a wave of relief. "That's wonderful. Thanks for letting me know."

"One of us will stop by tomorrow to pick you up if you want to see him," Mike continued.

"I'd like that, thanks." She disconnected from the call and closed her eyes, thanking God for giving Matt the strength to pull through surgery.

The welcome news about Matt helped her to relax enough to fall asleep. Rory woke up at 5:30 a.m. for a bottle. It was the longest he'd slept through the night since this nightmare had started. She fed him and let Duchess out. Since Rory showed no interest in going back to sleep, she stayed up, making a pot of coffee and helping herself to a slice of toast for breakfast.

Dawn crept over the horizon. She sipped her coffee, wondering how long they would keep Matt in the hospital. Probably a few days at the most, which meant she would need to find an alternative place to stay.

Not to mention she had things to do. Starting with filing the paperwork to adopt Rory and enrolling him in a day-care center. And looking for a new place to live.

She had to accept the fact that her time with Matt had come to an end. Matt needed to focus on recovering from his bullet wound and subsequent surgery. The last thing he needed was to deal with her and Rory. Especially after what he'd been through in his past.

And she needed to remember that her priority was Rory. Not Matt.

Lacy packed all her belongings into a small pile. Most of it belonged to Rory. Once she made sure Matt was truly all right, she would ask his brothers to take her home. Her apartment was small, but it would have to do for now.

The hours dragged by slowly, to the point where she was beginning to wonder if Mike and Miles had forgotten about her.

Had Matt's condition taken a turn for the worse?

No, someone would have called her. It was more likely they were continuing to discuss the case with the detective.

By ten o'clock in the morning, her worry had grown to astronomical proportions. She let Duchess out into the fenced-in backyard, then called both Mike and Miles, but neither one of them picked up.

Ten minutes later, she heard a car pull into the driveway. With a sense of relief, she set the disposable phone down and went over to greet one of Matt's brothers.

She opened the front door, expecting to see Mike or Miles. The moment she opened the door, Duchess let out a series of staccato barks from the backyard.

By the time she realized it wasn't one of Matt's brothers but a dark-haired stranger at the door, he'd pushed his way inside, holding a gun pointed at her chest.

And she knew, with a sick sense of certainty, that the danger was far from over.

"Let me up," Matt said, pushing Miles out of the way. "I'm getting out of here."

His brother let out a heavy sigh. "The doctor recommended you stay another day."

Matt reached for the crutches that were propped at the end of his bed. The wound in his thigh ached, especially when he'd pulled on the sweats his brother had brought in for him to wear, but he ignored it. "Yeah, but that was before you told me Styles thinks someone else is the brains behind the murder of David and Jill Williams.

That both Nichols and Whalen are refusing to give up the guy's identity. You shouldn't have left Lacy and Rory alone."

"Duchess will watch over them," Miles assured him. "But if you insist on leaving, I'm going to get the doctor. And you're going to explain this to Mom and Nan."

"Yeah, yeah." Matt vaguely remembered seeing his mother and grandmother standing at his bedside last night when he'd returned from surgery. Maddy and his other brothers had been there, too.

But he hadn't seen Lacy. Which had bothered him, far more than it should have.

Logically, he understood she had Rory to care for, but he didn't feel comfortable having her out of his sight. He knew the police were likely still grilling Nichols and Whalen to give up their source, but he didn't like thinking about someone still out there as a potential threat.

It was twenty minutes before ten in the morning. The surgeon had come by several hours earlier. Physical therapy had arrived by eight with the crutches, and once he was mobile, there was no reason to hang around.

And two very good reasons to leave: Lacy and Rory.

Despite his grumbling, Miles escorted him out to the car and helped him inside. Once they were on the road, Miles's phone rang. Since he was driving, Miles didn't bother to answer it.

"Give it to me," Matt said. "I'd like to call Lacy."

"Hang on a minute," Miles said. "I need to get on the interstate first."

Matt waited impatiently, then took the phone Miles finally handed over. "Hey, we just missed a call from Lacy."

"We did?" Miles looked surprised. "I wonder why she was reaching out to us?" Matt quickly called Lacy back. She didn't pick up. He tried not to panic, and just when he was going to try calling again, the phone rang in his hand. Unfortunately, the caller was Mike, not Lacy.

"This is Matt, what's going on?"

"I just missed a call from Lacy, so I'm heading over to your place," Mike said. "Have you heard from her?"

"No, my phone battery is dead. She tried to call Miles, too. We're on our way."

"Meet you there," Mike said and disconnected.

Matt gripped the phone tightly in his hand, nausea swirling in his gut. "Hurry, Miles."

Miles gave a terse nod and pushed his foot firmly on the accelerator.

Both of his brothers made good time. When Miles arrived, Mike was already pulling into the driveway of his small ranch house. There was a strange car parked on the street, and Duchess was barking like mad from the backyard. Matt reached over to grip Miles's arm.

"Someone's inside. I need a weapon. I'll go around back to get Duchess—you and Mike cover the front."

"Let me call for backup first." Miles wrestled the phone to make the call, then dug a second gun from the glove box.

Matt tucked the weapon into his waistband and then pushed open the passenger-side door. With the help of his crutches, he hobbled over to the backyard and used his key to open the lock on the fence.

Duchess came right over to greet him but didn't stay. She raced over to the back door leading into his house.

Matt hobbled—slowly on the crutches—over to the doorway, pausing long enough to take a deep breath. He listened intently and then used his key to unlock the door.

Duchess stayed close. He didn't hear anything from the front of the house, but he was sure his brothers were there, waiting. Matt propped his right crutch against the side of the house and pulled out his weapon. He'd have to make do with one crutch from here on. Moving silently, he eased inside, giving Duchess the Stay command to keep her close.

"I don't see how planting evidence here is going to work," Lacy said from the living room. "No one will believe Matt is responsible for blackmail and murder."

"I'm not going down for this," a male voice said. "Trust me, I have enough connections who will believe Callahan is responsible. Once he's dead and I get rid of you and the kid, I'll come out looking like a hero."

Matt peered around the corner in time to see Assistant District Attorney Blake Ratcliff standing there with a gun pointed at Lacy and Rory.

"Drop it, Blake!" he shouted. "Attack!"

Duchess shot out of the kitchen directly toward Blake. The ADA turned and took aim at the dog, so Matt pulled the trigger on his weapon, hitting Blake in the stomach and sending him stumbling backward. He hit the ground and Duchess planted her paws on Ratcliff's chest, as if determined to make sure he couldn't get back up again. His brothers burst in through the front door, and just that quickly, it was over.

For good this time.

"Matt? What are you doing out of the hospital?" Lacy ran toward him, her expression etched with concern. "Mike, Miles? Why did you bring him here? He needs to go back right away."

"I'm fine," he assured her, reaching out with his free hand to give her a hug. He vaguely remembered telling her that he loved her last night before he had fallen unconscious, but he couldn't remember if she'd responded.

"Who is he?" Lacy asked, glancing over her shoulder at the man stretched out on the floor.

"Assistant District Attorney Blake Ratcliff." Matt reluctantly let her go. "I knew he was trouble when Noah confided how he assaulted my sister, but I never expected this. He was crazy if he thought he could pin this all on me."

"When did he assault Maddy?" Miles asked with a frown.

Matt winced. "I'm not sure. She didn't tell me, Noah did. So don't say anything."

"Backup will be here shortly," Mike said. "I guess he was the brains behind the murders. Do you want to go back to the hospital?"

"No." He may as well stay. He would have to deal with Ratcliff, anyway. Then he caught sight of Lacy's things gathered together in a neat pile. "Why is all your stuff sitting there?"

Lacy shrugged, avoiding his gaze. "It's time for me to go home. I have a lot of things to do over the next few weeks."

"But I thought..." He wasn't sure what he'd thought. "Couldn't you wait until we have a chance to talk?"

"Matt, you've been wonderful. I can't thank you enough for helping me find strength in faith and in God. I know now, with God's help, Rory and I will be just fine."

He stared at her for several long seconds, trying to think of an argument that might change her mind. But what else was there to say? He'd already declared his love.

Clearly, she didn't feel the same way.

Mike's phone rang, and his brother quickly answered it. "Marc? What's wrong? Hey, stay calm, bro, Kari will be fine. We'll meet you at the hospital, okay?"

"Kari?" Matt asked, when Mike disconnected from the phone. "Is she all right?"

"She went into premature labor. The baby is three weeks early. Hopefully, Kari will be fine. Marc's a wreck, though."

"I don't blame him, but we can't just leave," Miles pointed out. "We have to explain what happened here."

"Call Detective Styles," Lacy suggested. "He'll understand."

The backup police officers arrived shortly thereafter, but Detective Styles didn't arrive for another twenty minutes. He wasn't surprised to see Ratcliff—apparently Whalen had finally broken down, confessing everything and implicating the ADA, who'd paid them to get the notebook at any cost.

Combined with the rest of the evidence that

Matt, Miles and Mike had gathered, the two officers involved would go to jail for a long time.

Finally, a good hour later, the Callahans were free to go.

"Lacy, will you please come with us to the hospital?" Matt asked. "For one thing, I can't drive, and we need to check on my brother and his wife before we take you home."

She hesitated, then nodded. "What about Duchess?"

"She's coming, too."

"Sounds good, but I'd like to take my things now, so we can head straight to my place when we're finished."

He wanted to argue, but his brothers helped gather her stuff together, putting it all into the back seat. Soon they were back at the hospital where the rest of the Callahan clan had already gathered in the waiting room.

"Kari and Marc are in the labor room," his mother announced. "This baby is determined to be born early, that's for sure."

Miles crossed over to his hugely pregnant wife, Paige. "Guess our baby isn't going to be born on the same day as Marc and Kari's," he said in a soft voice, placing his palm protectively over her abdomen.

"I guess not," Paige responded with a wry

grimace. "Although, I can't deny feeling a tiny bit jealous."

Matt shook his head. There were so many babies that he could barely keep up. Then again, the idea of having a ready-made family was growing on him.

Despite his intention to avoid complications, he'd fallen in love with Lacy. Somehow, he needed to find a way to convince her to give him a chance.

"I'd like to introduce you to my mother and grandmother," he told Lacy.

"Oh, well, okay…" Lacy looked uncertain as he gestured for his mother to join them.

"Mom, this is Lacy Germaine. Lacy, this is Margaret Callahan, my mother, and Nan, my grandmother."

"Nice to meet you," Lacy said with a small smile.

"You, too, dear. Oh, and who's this little cutie?" his mother asked, beaming at Rory.

"My orphaned nephew, Rory," Lacy answered. "I'm planning to adopt him."

"Oh, I'm so sorry for your loss." His mother gave Lacy a quick hug. "But I'm sure you'll be a great mother to Rory."

Lacy nodded with confidence. "Yes, I will."

Maddy crowded in, not one to be left out. "Hi,

Lacy, it's great to meet you. I've heard so much about you."

"You have?" Lacy appeared taken aback.

"Noah was there last night, remember?" Matt leaned heavily on his crutches, unwilling to admit how much he wanted to sit down.

"Oh, yes. Of course." Lacy's puzzled expression cleared. "It's nice to meet you, too, Maddy."

"It's a girl!" Marc's excited announcement echoed loudly throughout the waiting room. "Kari and I have a beautiful baby girl!"

"Oh, Marc, that's wonderful." Matt's mother rushed over to give her eldest son a hug. "What are you going to name her?"

Marc grinned. "Since our firstborn is Max after our dad, we decided to name our daughter Maggie after you."

"Oh, that's so sweet." Matt's mother's blue eyes filled with tears.

Matt groaned. "Don't tell me you're continuing on the *M* name madness," he protested. "It's crazy enough around here as it is!"

"Yep." Marc beamed. "But no worries, there will be plenty of *M* names to go around. I'm not sure Kari is up to having six kids."

"Yeah, and this probably isn't the right time to broach that subject with her, either," Mike added in a wry tone.

Matt coughed to cover up a laugh when his

mother swatted Mike on the arm. "Enough, young man."

It took him a minute to realize that Lacy was edging toward the door. Was she planning to leave without him?

He quickly followed her out of the waiting room. "Lacy, what's wrong?"

"Nothing." She subtly wiped at her eyes. Was she crying? "Your family is great, Matt. But I'm tired and need to get home."

"Lacy, wait." He walked over to her with his crutches and then leaned on his good leg so he could take her hand in his. "I know it's too soon for you, but I can't stand the thought of living my life without you. I love you. Will you please consider giving me—us—a chance?"

Her mouth dropped open in shock. "You...love me?"

"Didn't I tell you that last night?" When she shook her head, he inwardly groaned at his stupidity. "Yes, Lacy, I love you. And Rory, too. I know that there's a long adoption road ahead, but I want to be there with you, helping you, supporting you along the way. But most of all, I can't imagine not having you in my life."

"Oh, Matt." Lacy's eyes filled with tears. "As much as I would love to have your support, this isn't a good time to start a relationship. Being responsible for a baby will be stressful enough."

He swallowed hard and nodded. "Adapting to a baby won't be easy, but we managed pretty well so far, don't you think? And we can take things as slow as you'd like, but please, please don't leave without giving me a chance."

Lacy swiped at her eyes, then unexpectedly threw herself into his arms. He dropped his crutches to hold her close. Well, as close as possible considering she still held Rory.

"I love you, too, Matt," she murmured against his chest. "I've always felt safe with you, and not just from the men chasing us, but on a personal level. If you're really sure about this, I'd love to give our relationship a chance to flourish."

Matt's heart swelled with gratitude and love. "I knew God brought us together for a reason," he said, pressing a kiss to her temple.

She lifted her head and kissed him until they were both breathless. "Me, too," she whispered.

He continued to hold her, thrilled with the knowledge that the Callahan clan would soon expand by two more.

"Another Callahan bites the dust," a wry female voice said from the doorway.

He ignored the fact that his twin had thrown his own words back at him. She was right.

And he would show Lacy and Rory how much he loved them, every day for the rest of their lives.

EPILOGUE

Three months later

Church services followed by Sunday brunch with Matt's family had become Lacy's favorite way to end the week. Especially now that school was over for the summer.

The past few months had been amazing. Matt's support during the adoption process had been invaluable, and she knew deep in her heart that she would soon legally be Rory's mother.

She'd managed to get a service to clean up Jill's house so she could put it on the market. As much as she missed her sister, she knew Jill wouldn't mind. It was better for her and Rory to have a new place to start over in.

Exactly one week after Maggie was born, Miles and Paige welcomed a son, whom they named Adam. Abby was thrilled to be a big sister. Apparently, they were going to stick with *A* names, which she privately thought was a smart idea.

"That was delicious, Mom," Matt said, rising to his feet. His thigh incision had healed nicely, and he'd been cleared to return to full duty within the week.

"Yes, it was," Lacy agreed, jumping up to assist in clearing the table. "Thank you for including me and Rory."

"You're always welcome, dear," Margaret Callahan assured her with a knowing smile that never failed to make her blush. She was thankful the Callahans had been warm and welcoming, including both her and Rory in family gatherings.

"Noah and I will take cleanup duty," Maddy offered, taking the dirty plate from Lacy's hand. "I think you guys should take advantage of this beautiful day."

"Oh, it's fine, really…" Lacy was about to protest, but Matt came over to put his arm around her waist.

"Thanks, sis. Come on, Lacy, let's take Rory to the park. You know how much he loves the baby swings."

Leaving the mess for everyone else to deal with didn't sit well with her, but Matt was insistent. He pushed her gently toward the door, stopping long enough to raise Rory up into his arms.

Outside, the sunshine was bright and she grabbed Matt's arm to stop him. "Wait, we need Rory's hat."

"Got it right here." He pulled a blue baseball cap out of his back pocket and tugged it on over Rory's fine blond hair.

She smiled, knowing that she shouldn't be surprised by Matt's conscientiousness. He'd proven to be a great father figure for Rory.

And he'd been wonderful toward her as well. He'd never raised his voice in anger. If he grew frustrated, he insisted they sit down to talk things out. He'd shown her what being in a normal relationship was really like.

She loved that about him. In fact, she loved everything about him.

They walked to the park where Matt placed Rory in the baby swing, making sure he was securely buckled in before giving him a push.

Rory laughed in glee, enjoying every minute of swinging back and forth beneath the blue sky. At six months old, he was crawling, and she felt sure walking wasn't far off, either. Then things would really get interesting.

"Are you ready to head back to work?" Lacy asked, as Matt turned toward her.

He nodded, somewhat absently. "Sure, why not?"

"No nightmares about being shot?" she asked.

"Not at all." He gave Rory another big push, then abruptly turned toward her. "Lacy Germaine, I love you. Will you please do me the honor of becoming my wife?"

She gaped at him in surprise, and he winced.

"I did it wrong," he muttered, dropping down onto one knee. He pulled out a small velvet ring box. "I'm sorry, let me try this again. Lacy Germaine, I love you with all my heart. Will you please marry me?"

"Yes." She laughed and tugged him up to his feet. "Yes, Matt, of course, I'll marry you. I love you, too. I'd be honored to become a part of the infamous Callahan family."

Matt pulled her close, sealing the deal with a deep kiss.

Lacy kissed him back, knowing there was no better man on the face of the earth for her and for Rory.

She cherished becoming a Callahan for real.

* * * * *

*If you enjoyed this story,
look for the other books in the*
CALLAHAN CONFIDENTIAL *series:*

*SHIELDING HIS CHRISTMAS WITNESS
THE ONLY WITNESS
CHRISTMAS AMNESIA*

*And pick up these other exciting stories
from Laura Scott:*

*WRONGLY ACCUSED
DOWN TO THE WIRE
UNDER THE LAWMAN'S PROTECTION
FORGOTTEN MEMORIES
HOLIDAY ON THE RUN
MIRROR IMAGE*

Available now from Love Inspired Suspense!

*Find more great reads at
www.LoveInspired.com*

Dear Reader,

Shattered Lullaby is the fourth book in my Callahan Confidential miniseries. I appreciate all of you who wrote to me letting me know how much you're enjoying my Callahan series. This book revolves around Maddy's twin, Matthew Callahan, and his K-9 partner, Duchess.

When Matt and Duchess come upon a crime in progress, he doesn't hesitate to step in to assist the woman carrying a three-month-old baby. As the gunman continues to stalk them, it soon becomes clear that Lacy Germaine has witnessed something big the night she escaped with her infant nephew, Rory. And the men determined to find her to silence her once and for all have deep ties in the police community.

I hope you enjoy Matt and Lacy's story as I continue to work diligently on the next book in my Callahan Confidential series. I love hearing from my readers. If you're interested in contacting me or signing up for my newsletter, please visit my website at www.laurascottbooks.com. I'm also on Facebook at Laura Scott Books Author and on Twitter @Laurascottbooks.

Yours in faith,
Laura Scott

Get 2 Free Books,
<u>Plus</u> 2 Free Gifts—
just for trying the Reader Service!

YES! Please send me 2 FREE Love Inspired® Romance novels and my 2 FREE mystery gifts (gifts are worth about $10 retail). After receiving them, if I don't wish to receive any more books, I can return the shipping statement marked "cancel." If I don't cancel, I will receive 6 brand-new novels every month and be billed just $5.24 for the regular-print edition or $5.74 each for the larger-print edition in the U.S., or $5.74 each for the regular-print edition or $6.24 each for the larger-print edition in Canada. That's a saving of at least 13% off the cover price. It's quite a bargain! Shipping and handling is just 50¢ per book in the U.S. and 75¢ per book in Canada.* I understand that accepting the 2 free books and gifts places me under no obligation to buy anything. I can always return a shipment and cancel at any time. The free books and gifts are mine to keep no matter what I decide.

Please check one:
☐ Love Inspired Romance Regular-Print (105/305 IDN GMWU)
☐ Love Inspired Romance Larger-Print (122/322 IDN GMWU)

Name _____ (PLEASE PRINT)

Address _____ Apt. #

City _____ State/Province _____ Zip/Postal Code

Signature (if under 18, a parent or guardian must sign)

Mail to the **Reader Service:**
IN U.S.A.: P.O. Box 1341, Buffalo, NY 14240-8531
IN CANADA: P.O. Box 603, Fort Erie, Ontario L2A 5X3

Want to try two free books from another line?
Call 1-800-873-8635 today or visit www.ReaderService.com.

*Terms and prices subject to change without notice. Prices do not include applicable taxes. Sales tax applicable in N.Y. Canadian residents will be charged applicable taxes. Offer not valid in Quebec. This offer is limited to one order per household. Books received may not be as shown. Not valid for current subscribers to Love Inspired Romance books. All orders subject to approval. Credit or debit balances in a customer's account(s) may be offset by any other outstanding balance owed by or to the customer. Please allow 4 to 6 weeks for delivery. Offer available while quantities last.

Your Privacy—The Reader Service is committed to protecting your privacy. Our Privacy Policy is available online at www.ReaderService.com or upon request from the Reader Service.
We make a portion of our mailing list available to reputable third parties that offer products we believe may interest you. If you prefer that we not exchange your name with third parties, or if you wish to clarify or modify your communication preferences, please visit us at www.ReaderService.com/consumerschoice or write to us at Reader Service Preference Service, P.O. Box 9062, Buffalo, NY 14240-9062. Include your complete name and address.

LI17R3

Get 2 Free Books,
Plus 2 Free Gifts—
just for trying the Reader Service!

HARLEQUIN
HEARTWARMING™

YES! Please send me 2 FREE Harlequin® Heartwarming™ Larger-Print novels and my 2 FREE mystery gifts (gifts worth about $10 retail). After receiving them, if I don't wish to receive any more books, I can return the shipping statement marked "cancel." If I don't cancel, I will receive 4 brand-new larger-print novels every month and be billed just $5.49 per book in the U.S. or $6.24 per book in Canada. That's a savings of at least 19% off the cover price. It's quite a bargain! Shipping and handling is just 50¢ per book in the U.S. and 75¢ per book in Canada*. I understand that accepting the 2 free books and gifts places me under no obligation to buy anything. I can always return a shipment and cancel at any time. The free books and gifts are mine to keep no matter what I decide.

161/361 IDN GMWQ

Name	(PLEASE PRINT)

Address	Apt. #

City	State/Prov.	Zip/Postal Code

Signature (if under 18, a parent or guardian must sign)

Mail to the **Reader Service:**
IN U.S.A.: P.O. Box 1341, Buffalo, NY 14240-8531
IN CANADA: P.O. Box 603, Fort Erie, Ontario L2A 5X3

Want to try two free books from another line?
Call 1-800-873-8635 today or visit www.ReaderService.com.

*Terms and prices subject to change without notice. Prices do not include applicable taxes. Sales tax applicable in N.Y. Canadian residents will be charged applicable taxes. Offer not valid in Quebec. This offer is limited to one order per household. Books received may not be as shown. Not valid for current subscribers to Harlequin Heartwarming Larger-Print books. All orders subject to approval. Credit or debit balances in a customer's account(s) may be offset by any other outstanding balance owed by or to the customer. Please allow 4 to 6 weeks for delivery. Offer available while quantities last.

Your Privacy—The Reader Service is committed to protecting your privacy. Our Privacy Policy is available online at www.ReaderService.com or upon request from the Reader Service.

We make a portion of our mailing list available to reputable third parties that offer products we believe may interest you. If you prefer that we not exchange your name with third parties, or if you wish to clarify or modify your communication preferences, please visit us at www.ReaderService.com/consumerschoice or write to us at Reader Service Preference Service, P.O. Box 9062, Buffalo, NY 14240-9062. Include your complete name and address.

HWI17R2

HOMETOWN HEARTS ♥

YES! Please send me **The Hometown Hearts Collection** in Larger Print. This collection begins with 3 FREE books and 2 FREE gifts in the first shipment. Along with my 3 free books, I'll also get the next 4 books from the Hometown Hearts Collection, in LARGER PRINT, which I may either return and owe nothing, or keep for the low price of $4.99 U.S./ $5.89 CDN each plus $2.99 for shipping and handling per shipment*. If I decide to continue, about once a month for 8 months I will get 6 or 7 more books, but will only need to pay for 4. That means 2 or 3 books in every shipment will be FREE! If I decide to keep the entire collection, I'll have paid for only 32 books because 19 books are FREE! I understand that accepting the 3 free books and gifts places me under no obligation to buy anything. I can always return a shipment and cancel at any time. My free books and gifts are mine to keep no matter what I decide.

262 HCN 3432 462 HCN 3432

Name	(PLEASE PRINT)	
Address		Apt. #
City	State/Prov.	Zip/Postal Code

Signature (if under 18, a parent or guardian must sign)

Mail to the **Reader Service:**
IN U.S.A.: P.O. Box 1867, Buffalo, NY. 14240-1867
IN CANADA: P.O. Box 609, Fort Erie, Ontario L2A 5X3

* Terms and prices subject to change without notice. Prices do not include applicable taxes. Sales tax applicable in NY. Canadian residents will be charged applicable taxes. This offer is limited to one order per household. All orders subject to approval. Credit or debit balances in a customer's account(s) may be offset by any other outstanding balance owed by or to the customer. Please allow 4 to 6 weeks for delivery. Offer available while quantities last. Offer not available to Quebec residents.

> **Your Privacy**—The Reader Service is committed to protecting your privacy. Our Privacy Policy is available online at www.ReaderService.com or upon request from the Reader Service.
>
> We make a portion of our mailing list available to reputable third parties that offer products we believe may interest you. If you prefer that we not exchange your name with third parties, or if you wish to clarify or modify your communication preferences, please visit us at www.ReaderService.com/consumerschoice or write to us at Reader Service Preference Service, P.O. Box 9062, Buffalo, NY. 14240-9062. Include your complete name and address.

HHBPA17

READERSERVICE.COM

Manage your account online!

- Review your order history
- Manage your payments
- Update your address

> *We've designed the*
> *Reader Service website*
> *just for you.*

Enjoy all the features!

- Discover new series available to you, and read excerpts from any series.
- Respond to mailings and special monthly offers.
- Browse the Bonus Bucks catalog and online-only exculsives.
- Share your feedback.

Visit us at:

ReaderService.com

RS16R